LEADING LADIES

READ MORE ABOUT MEGAN

Deaf Child Crossing by Marlee Matlin

Nobody's Perfect by Marlee Matlin
and Doug Cooney

MARLEE MATLIN
&
DOUG COONEY

LEADING LADIES

SIMON & SCHUSTER BOOKS
FOR YOUNG READERS

NEW YORK LONDON TORONTO SYDNEY

SIMON & SCHUSTER BOOKS FOR YOUNG READERS
An imprint of Simon & Schuster Children's Publishing Division
1230 Avenue of the Americas, New York, New York 10020
This book is a work of fiction. Any references to historical events, real people, or real locales are used fictitiously. Other names, characters, places, and incidents are products of the author's imagination, and any resemblance to actual events or locales or persons, living or dead, is entirely coincidental.

SIMON & SCHUSTER BOOKS FOR YOUNG READERS is a trademark of Simon & Schuster, Inc.
Book design by Al Cetta
The text for this book is set in Baskerville.
Signs (page 278) from *The Joy of Signing* by Lottie L. Riekehof, Gospel Publishing House, copyright © 1987. Used by permission.
Manufactured in the United States of America
2 4 6 8 10 9 7 5 3 1
Library of Congress Cataloging-in-Publication Data
Matlin, Marlee.
Leading ladies / Marlee Matlin and Doug Cooney.—1st ed.
p. cm.
Summary: A deaf fourth-grader finds her true calling when she is cast as Dorothy in a school production of *The Wizard of Oz*.
ISBN-13: 978-0-689-86987-7 (hardcover : alk. paper)
ISBN-10: 0-689-86987-8 (hardcover : alk. paper)
[1. Deaf—Fiction. 2. People with disabilities—Fiction. 3. Theater—Fiction. 4. Acting—Fiction. 5. Schools—Fiction.] I. Cooney, Doug.
II. Title.
PZ7.M4312Le 2007
[Fic]—dc22
2006031573

FIRST
EDITION

ACKNOWLEDGMENTS

There are several people I would like to thank. Once again, many thanks to to my agent, the ever-patient Alan Nevins. I would also like to thank my editor, the wonderful David Gale, and everyone at Simon & Schuster.

In addition there are a few others without whom this book would not have been possible. To my husband, Kevin, and my children, Sarah, Brandon, Tyler, and Isabelle, thank you for all your patience, love and support. To my friends and to my original BFF, Liz Tannebaum, who inspired many of the stories in this book, thank you. And to Jack Jason, my business partner for the last twenty-one years—thank you for all the compassionate work you put out there on my behalf.

Finally, this book would have not been possible without my brilliant writing partner, Doug Cooney. As I've said before, you helped bring Megan to life for more adventures and for that I am forever grateful.—M. M.

ACKNOWLEDGMENTS

Without Marlee Matlin's warmth, wisdom, humor, and spirit, this book would not have been possible. I also thank Jack Jason and my editors at Simon & Schuster Books for Young Readers, David Gale and Alexandra Cooper, for their insights, guidance, and support—as well as Claire Blanchard for her gracious introduction to American Sign Language.—D. C.

ONE
POLKA DOT

"Left, right-left, *hop*! Right, left-right, *hop*!" Ms. Endee called in the school gymnasium, using a snappy rhythm. "If you're facing opposite, you have to do the reverse! Left, right-left, *again*! Right, left-right, *again*!"

Megan looked at her friend Cindy and screwed her face into a question mark. "What?"

"It's left-right-left, hop," Cindy repeated, using speech and sign language. "And the same thing on the other side. Right, left, right. And then hop." Cindy tried the step herself but Megan didn't budge. Instead she gazed around the room at the sight of all her classmates hopping, flopping, and skipping side to side.

"Everybody has ants in their pants!" said Megan.

Cindy laughed a little and grabbed Megan's hand. "Come on, follow me! It's better to learn the dance than to stand there catching flies!" She imitated Megan's open mouth and her slack-jawed expression.

Megan immediately closed her mouth and smirked. "You're right," she agreed, squaring off with Cindy. "Let's dance!"

Every February, Ms. Endee dedicated a segment of time in her fourth-grade classroom to Folk Dances of Many Nations. It was an unofficial annual tradition at Wilmot Elementary. Most of Ms. Endee's current fourth-grade class knew the day was coming from listening to kids in the playground from the year before. Even so, the scene in the school gymnasium was the usual chaos.

The students formed two great big circles and each kid faced off with the one standing opposite, as Ms. Endee instructed. Of course, a lot of them were wiggling and chattering and not paying any attention to Ms. Endee's instructions either.

The fact that there were more girls than boys in their class meant that Megan had to rescue Cindy from partnering with Tony Rosenblum. "You're dancing with *me*," she said, snatching Cindy's hand and placing her other hand at Cindy's waist so that they were locked into dance position. Tony Rosenblum ended up dancing with their friend Alexis, a tall, pretty, and supersmart girl who was relatively new at Wilmot Elementary. Alexis Powell was a good sport about dancing with Tony—even though she stood a good three inches above him.

Once the students had tackled the basic "left, right-left, *hop*," Ms. Endee turned on the portable boom box from the classroom. "Now try it again, a little faster," she cried, "and this time to music!" She clapped her hands loudly, in big broad gestures, emphatically marking the loud "oompah-oompah" wafting from the CD player.

Being deaf, Megan couldn't exactly hear the music. She wore hearing aids so she could sort of hear something, especially something really loud as the music was now. She didn't hear music the way other kids listen to the radio or iPods or CD players—but Megan knew well enough what music was. In fact, she had a good sense of rhythm. And if the music was as loud as it was in the gym, she could feel the sound vibrations coming through the floor. Other kids might have felt the sound vibrations too—but they didn't notice or appreciate them the same way because they didn't happen to be deaf.

In the classroom, Megan relied on Jann, her sign language interpreter, to translate everything that was going on. Other times—both inside the classroom and out—Megan preferred to get the translation from her best friend, Cindy.

"Ready, set, go," said Cindy. "Come on, Megan, we're dancing!" Both girls gamely hopped through the steps from left to right, over and over and over.

Megan freed a hand to wag by her ear and looked quizzically at Cindy. "So what's this music?" she asked.

Cindy didn't answer the question with words. She pursed her lips, crossed her eyes, and puffed her cheeks, pretending to blast into an imaginary tuba.

Megan laughed out loud. "What are you doing?"

"It's a *tuba*," said Cindy. She freed one hand to spell the word

T U B A

"*T-U-B-A*," using the manual alphabet.

"Tuba!" she repeated, exaggerating her lips as she enunciated both syllables because she knew that Megan was a lip-reader, too.

"What the heck is a 'tuba'?" Megan replied, twisting her mouth to imitate Cindy's funny face.

"It's a big musical instrument that—" Cindy began but stopped because she had just landed directly on Megan's foot.

"Oww!" cried Megan, stopping to grab her foot and put on a big show. "You stepped on my foot!"

"It's *your* fault," said Cindy distractedly. "You asked me about the *tuba!*" They shook out their hands and resumed their position to start the dance all over again.

"A tuba must be loud," said Megan, once they got the hang of the steps.

"How can you tell?" asked Cindy.

"From the vibrations in the floor," Megan replied. She stopped to press her sneaker flat against the floor.

And that was when Cindy stepped on Megan's foot for the second time.

"Owwwwwww!" cried Megan, maybe a little louder than was necessary. "You're not a very good dancer!"

"I'm a great dancer!" Cindy protested.

"It's your fault! You put your foot under my foot when you stopped dancing!"

"Let's take a break anyway," said Megan, willing to let it go. "I need to catch my breath."

Glancing about the room, Megan and Cindy saw that most of their classmates were doing pretty well with the side-step part of the dance. Alexis and Tony Rosenblum in particular seemed to be having a lot of fun. As it turned out, Tony was a pretty good dancer.

"Nice moves, Tony," said Megan, as the two of them drew near.

"My mom taught me," Tony replied, somewhat embarrassed at his own ability. He and Alexis paused to take a quick breather alongside Megan and Cindy. "My mom insisted. She rolled up the rug in the living room and everything. I told her everybody would tease me."

"We're not teasing you," said Megan.

"No, no, no," added Cindy, "we're very impressed."

"Tony and I have to keep practicing," said Alexis. "He dances so well that he's making me look bad!"

"You don't look bad," said Tony, leading

Alexis back onto the dance floor. "You do the steps right, but you have to stop looking at your feet!"

Megan and Cindy continued to watch as Tony and Alexis started dancing again. "Look at Tony go," said Cindy. "I'd be better off dancing with Tony Rosenblum."

"But you're stuck with me," said Megan, tugging Cindy's hand to pull her back into position. "Deal with it."

Megan and Cindy grew more confident as they practiced the steps—left, right-left, *hop!*—to the "oompah" music. As soon as they got comfortable with the dance steps, of course, Ms. Endee made the dance a little more complicated. "Okay, boys and girls!" she announced in her big voice. "Start *turning!* Everybody, get ready to turn! Ready, set, *turn!*"

The entire dance floor came to a screeching halt.

"Wha-aat?" the kids cried. Either the kids hadn't heard what she'd said over the music, didn't understand what she meant, or simply couldn't believe it. Regardless, a whole smattering of kids bluntly refused to budge. Dancers pulled partners to a standstill, peppered with loud groans of dismay and disbelief. Everyone was completely thrown by the prospect of where-and-when-and-how-and-whom to *turn*.

Except for Tony Rosenblum, of course. "I told you we were going to have to turn," he said to Alexis.

"Ms. Endee!" Alexis cried loudly. "How are we possibly supposed to *turn*?"

"What is the problem?" the teacher replied with a small chuckle. "I ask for a simple turn—and you act like I said, 'Stand on your head!'"

"Oh! I can stand on my head!" cried Casey Waite, raising her hand. Several other budding gymnasts threw their hands in the air as well.

"Thanks for offering, Casey," Ms. Endee replied, "but we don't need to see you stand on your head again." She turned toward Jann, Megan's sign interpreter. "Jann," she said, extending her hand, "would you care to join me on the dance floor?"

"I'd be delighted," Jann replied.

The children giggled as Ms. Endee and Jann stepped into the middle of the room as dance partners. The two women took their positions and began the little side-step shuffle to the music. "Watch closely!" Ms. Endee called out, as she and Jann marked the movement. "Every time you *hop*, you also *turn*. Ready? Set? Starting *now*!"

At the next opportunity, Ms. Endee and Jann began hopping and *turning* around each other in little circles on the dance floor, never once missing the next step or landing on each other's foot. It was almost a gallop, really—and the little gallops rolled into a much larger gallop that took them all the way around the gymnasium floor, somehow managing to sidestep *and* hop *and* turn, all at the same time. The kids roared with approval. Ms. Endee and Jann laughed over their own dancing. After one full round, they released each other and turned toward the students with quick curtsies and bows.

"Now you try," Ms. Endee said encouragingly. "Come on! Give it a shot! You'll never know until you try!"

Jann approached Megan and Cindy for a brief huddle. "Do you girls understand?" she asked in sign.

"I think so," said Megan. "It looks like fun."

Cindy nodded in agreement.

"Okay, show us what you got," Jann

enthused—and ran back to the far corner of the gym where she could watch the action without getting trampled.

Megan and Cindy eagerly squeezed each other's palms in time to the beat.

"You know I'm going to step on your foot," said Cindy.

"Bring it on," said Megan, moving into position. "I'm ready this time!"

Ms. Endee turned on the "oompah" music and clapped the beat until the students were comfortable with the side-step shuffle again. Then she cried, "And now, *turn!*"

At her command, kids galloped—and continued to gallop and kept galloping—until they had galloped all the way around the room. It seemed impossible at first but as each couple gathered its own momentum, the prospect of turning wasn't so bad. If one dancer managed the turn, he or she pulled the partner along. Pretty soon, they were flinging one another about with relative ease. Mostly, the kids found themselves so surprised they hadn't fallen to the ground that they laughed at their own success or failure.

Tony Rosenblum and Alexis were turning so fast that Tony lost his glasses. Alexis managed to retrieve them before they got stomped in the horde of kids. She handed them back to him, he put them on, and they resumed the dance position. "More?" said Tony. "It's a jungle out there."

"Let's do it," said Alexis.

Megan and Cindy were doing really very well with the polka—until Megan tried to get tricky and switch direction. Naturally, Cindy landed right on Megan's foot again.

"*Owwwwwwww!*" Megan howled, even more dramatically than before. She stopped in her tracks and leaned over to rub her foot.

"Did I hurt you?" asked Cindy, stopping to look down as well.

"Not really," said Megan, "I was just *acting.*" Glancing toward Cindy, she noticed a frenzied crunch of kids circling the floor—and headed right for them. Megan and Cindy were directly in the path of oncoming polka traffic. Megan quickly yanked Cindy to the side of the dance floor to avoid collisions—where they laughed, screamed, and caught their breath.

"Close call," said Cindy from the sidelines.

"You owe me," Megan replied. "I saved your life!"

"More?" said Cindy, resuming the dance position.

"More!" said Megan, yanking her partner back onto the floor.

With all the laughter and energy it took to do the polka, almost all the students were quickly winded—but the polka charged forward, and the excitement continued to climb. If a couple messed up or tripped over their own feet, they dove right back in. Nobody gave up until everyone was on the dance floor—*dancing*.

"I told you!" cried Ms. Endee, delighted with the results.

By the time the song ended, the entire fourth grade had the hang of the dance. They gave a big cheer and a huge round of applause, clapping for their partners, the music, and the whole class at large.

"That was a blast!" said Megan, leaning toward Cindy's ear. "This tuba dance is crazy!"

"It's not the 'tuba dance,'" Cindy replied. "It's called the polka."

"Spell it," said Megan.

Cindy released a hand to spell "*P-O-L-K-A.*"

P O L K A

"Pol-ka," Megan repeated, enunciating each syllable.

"Did we all enjoy that?" asked Ms. Endee, as the noise level simmered down. Megan's hand shot into the air. "Yes, Megan," her teacher replied.

"What's the difference between the 'polka' and the 'polka *dot*'?" Megan asked.

The class laughed as though the question was silly but Ms. Endee answered it all the same. "Good question," said Ms. Endee. "The polka craze hit the United States in 1840 or so. '*Polka*' is Polish for 'a Polish lady' and 'pulka' means 'half' in Czech, so it's anybody's guess how the dance was named. The dance was so popular that people would buy anything with the word 'polka' attached to it—even crazy fabric covered with dots—and that's how we got the 'polka dot'!"

Jann translated Ms. Endee's response into sign language so that Megan would be sure to understand.

"So the polka was like disco?" asked Tony Rosenblum.

"Like disco," said Ms. Endee, "like hip-hop, like rap."

It cracked the kids up that Ms. Endee referred to hip-hop and rap.

"But where did the polka come from?" asked Megan.

"The polka is danced all over the world," Ms. Endee explained, "but the dance itself probably originated in the Czech Republic, or more specifically in a country that doesn't actually exist anymore called Czechoslovakia."

"Oh, boy," Cindy muttered under her breath. "*Czechoslovakia*?! Watch this!" She turned her attention toward Jann, Megan's sign interpreter. Cindy was not alone. The entire class enjoyed watching Jann scramble through challenging translations of difficult phrases, complicated ideas, and really hard spelling words. They shifted their gaze toward Jann to see how she was going to handle "Czechoslovakia." Even Ms. Endee glanced over in anticipation.

Sure enough, when Jann arrived at the tricky word, she shifted from sign language into the manual alphabet and slowed her movements down slightly to make sure she got every letter correct.

C Z E C H O S L O V A K I A

At the end, Jann wiped her brow with a loud "whew" and shook her tired hands with relief. The students gave her a nice round of applause.

"You know, boys and girls, I've been thinking," said Ms. Endee. "We had such a huge success with the polka today that maybe we should put on a big demonstration for the whole school! How would you like that, huh? We could invite your parents, family, and friends to attend! How about a show of hands? How many people would like to do that?"

Ms. Endee seemed to be the only person who thought it was a good idea. Most kids felt okay making fools of themselves in phys. ed.— at least, every once in a while. But who wanted to suffer the same embarrassment in front of the whole school? Apparently, no one. Not a single hand was raised.

Well, not at first. A split-second after Jann finished the sign language translation of Ms. Endee's request, Megan's hand shot into the air.

"Megan?" asked Ms. Endee. "Megan is the only one? Nobody else wants to perform the polka for family and friends?"

"Let Megan do a solo!" cried Ronnie Jiu, trying to be funny as usual. "A solo for Megan!

I'd like to see that!" The entire class laughed.

"What did he say?" asked Megan, reacting to the laughter that was obvious on the faces around her.

"He said you could do a 'solo,'" Ms. Endee explained. "It was only a little joke. Ronnie wasn't being mean."

"Okay—but what's a 'solo'?" asked Megan.

"It means when you're out there all by yourself," Cindy explained. "Just you. Nobody else. That's a solo."

Out there by myself, thought Megan. *Sounds good to me.* "So what's wrong with that?" she asked out loud. Between the sign language and spoken word, she made herself heard. "What's so funny about a solo?" The class responded with a burst of outrageous laughter as though Megan had just said the funniest thing.

"I'm serious," Megan protested, repeating the question. "What's wrong with me dancing all by myself?"

Her class laughed louder still.

It seemed as if this situation happened all the time. Whenever Megan asked what she thought was a perfectly reasonable question, everybody laughed.

TWO
SIGN LANGUAGE

Megan and her mother, Lainee, had their own form of sign language. When Megan got home from school that day, she wanted to tell her mother about that awkward moment after the polka—when all the kids had laughed and she felt a little lonely, different, and weird.

Instead of searching for the words in sign language, Megan sat on a kitchen stool and slumped across the counter. Her arm sprawled so that her knuckles knocked into the bread box. Her face pressed against the tiles so that one cheek smooshed and her lips puckered. Her legs dangled off the stool like a discarded rag doll, and her weight rocked the stool on its legs as though it might tumble to the ground at any moment.

Her whole body turned into a pathetic little sigh.

It worked. Lainee turned from the sink, took one look at Megan—and said, "Okay—what?"

Megan shrugged and let her focus wander in another direction—which was her sign for "I don't want to talk about it but keep asking me questions."

Lainee reached for a bunch of white grapes, ran them under a quick blast of water in the sink, bundled them in a paper towel, and dropped them on the counter. She dragged a kitchen stool opposite Megan and pulled her daughter upright so that they were sitting knee-to-knee.

"Something's going on," said Lainee. "Tell me what it is."

Megan tugged a grape from the bunch and popped it into her mouth. She looked directly at her mother and let her eyes go blank—and then she began to chew.

"Is it school?" asked Lainee.

Megan scratched her cheek.

"Kids at school?" asked Lainee.

Megan shrugged. She plucked another grape, bit it in two, and studied the half that remained between her fingers.

"You're lonely, maybe? Misunderstood?" said Lainee.

Megan didn't want to say yes too quickly but she did want to let her mother know that she was warm. She sat up on the stool, let the grape wander to the opposite cheek—and continued to chew.

"Did somebody say something to upset you?"

Megan stopped chewing—which was a sign for "yes."

"Do you want to tell me what they said?"

Megan started chewing again—which was a sign for "no."

"Megan, honey," said her mother, smacking the counter in frustration, "I'm not playing Twenty Questions! Please stop sulking and just tell me what's wrong! You know I love you, but it drives me crazy when you won't speak your mind!"

Megan didn't hold it in a moment longer. "Kids laughed at me!" she blurted—both in sign and speech.

Her mother was quiet but only for a moment. "Oh, I see," she said. She reached for a grape to pop into her mouth. "And were you being silly?"

"No!" Megan erupted with indignation.

"*Mom*! I was being absolutely *serious* and everybody *laughed* at me!"

"Well, you can be silly sometimes so it wasn't a completely stupid question," her mother replied evenly. "Do you want to tell me what happened?"

Megan fingered a grape but didn't tug it from the bunch. "We were learning the polka," she said, "and Ms. Endee said we should do the polka for the whole school—but I was the only one who wanted to dance. Somebody said I should do a 'solo'—which means doing the polka all by myself, which is stupid because you dance the polka with a partner—but anyway I said, 'What's wrong with that? What's wrong with a solo? Why can't I dance all by myself?' And that's when everybody *laughed at me*."

Lainee let a moment pass before she spoke. Even then, all she said was, "Aw, honey."

"You think it's funny, too," said Megan.

"Am I laughing?" her mother replied. "You know I would *never* laugh at you. I would *love* to see you dance a solo. Polka or otherwise. Anytime!"

"So why were they laughing?" asked Megan.

"Maybe it was fun to imagine you dancing all by yourself," her mom replied. "Maybe they were laughing because they were delighted."

Megan looked down her nose at her mother. "You don't seriously believe that," she said.

"Maybe," her mom continued. "I don't know; I wasn't there! All I know is that you can't worry about what other people think. You'll drive yourself crazy that way. What you need to do is to be like the army!"

"Be like the army?" asked Megan.

"'Be all that you can be!'" said Lainee. "All you can do is to be you."

"But I'm already me," said Megan. "Who else could I be?"

"I meant like—be the best you can be," said her mother.

"They were laughing because I'm deaf," said Megan.

"I don't think that's true," her mother said quickly.

"Then because I'm different," Megan argued.

"We're all different," said her mother, giving up on the grapes.

"Not different like me," said Megan.

"You know what I think?" her mother suggested. "I think you should get on the computer and have a good talk with Lizzie, your friend from summer camp."

Megan smiled. She always smiled at the thought of Lizzie, this great girl that she and Cindy had met at summer camp. Lizzie also happened to be deaf but she didn't have the ability to speak, as Megan did. Lizzie spoke only sign language but they both read lips. Not surprisingly, Megan and Lizzie became fast friends—which made Megan's best friend Cindy uncomfortable at first, but now they all got along. Unfortunately, Lizzie lived in Long Grove, a suburb on the absolute other side of the city than the suburb where Megan lived, almost an hour away. Lizzie attended the Illinois School for the Deaf, an all-deaf school, so she and Megan almost never had a chance to get together. Even so, they spoke often enough using the computer.

Megan was always happy to hop on the computer, but she still didn't understand how that was going to help her problem. "Why call Lizzie?" she asked her mom. "Lizzie wasn't at my school today. She doesn't know what happened. What is Lizzie going to tell me?"

"It always makes you happy when you talk to Lizzie," her mother urged. "And I hate to see you feeling so down." She ran her hand across Megan's face and gently stroked her hair. "Besides," she continued, "I bet Lizzie has been blue a few times too. I bet she's had a few days when she was tired of seeming different and felt out there all by herself. If you talk to Lizzie, maybe you won't feel quite so 'solo.'"

Megan didn't respond, but she smiled a little bit. Gradually she straightened up on the kitchen stool. She hadn't even spoken with Lizzie yet—but she already felt better.

"Hit the computer," said Lainee, slapping her daughter's knee. "I have to get supper ready." As Lainee moved toward the refrigerator, Lizzie hopped off the stool and headed for the alcove where they kept the family computer. "Oh, and honey?" Lainee added, flagging her daughter's attention. "When your father gets home and asks if you learned anything at school today? I wouldn't mention the polka. I mean, he'd be happy to hear about the polka—but be sure to tell him what you learned in math, science, grammar, or something like that."

"Daddy doesn't like the polka?" asked Megan.

"It's not that he doesn't like the polka," Lainee hedged. "It's just that your father gets so crazy worrying that you'll be ready for college that he'd rather hear about the stuff going into your *brain*. You know! The serious stuff!"

"We learned the polka came from Czechoslovakia," Megan offered. She made a little performance out of spelling all the letters in "Czechoslovakia" correctly with the manual alphabet.

"Oh, yes, excellent!" Lainee replied. "Say 'Czechoslovakia' and then spell it for him! That'll make him so proud! He'll talk about that for days!"

Megan opened her instant message account and clicked on the rubber ducky icon that connected to Lizzie's screen name. A new box opened with a camera icon in the upper right corner.

Megan checked the camera on top of the computer monitor. The green light indicated that everything was working. Moments later, a new window opened and a video image of Lizzie popped into the frame.

"Hey, girl!" Lizzie signed. "You caught me doing homework in my bedroom!" Megan could tell Lizzie was sitting in her bedroom from the tiny video screen.

"Well, get rid of that pencil and talk to me," Megan signed back.

Lizzie leaned the tip of her pencil on the corner of her mouth and pretended to chomp on it, gobbling away, while she was actually inching the pencil into the palm of her hand. When the pencil disappeared, Lizzie wiped the corners of her mouth as though she had actually eaten the whole thing.

"Girl, you are so crazy!" Megan signed, even as she chuckled.

"You *told* me to get rid of the pencil!" Lizzie protested in mock alarm.

"I miss you!" Megan signed. "You make me laugh!"

"You always make me laugh too," Lizzie signed back. "And, boy-oh-boy, do I have a big surprise for you!"

"I hate surprises!" said Megan, delighted.

"Then you're really going to hate this one!" said Lizzie.

"Tell me! What is it?"

"I'm not going to tell you and ruin the

surprise!" Lizzie replied. "I've said too much! I'm changing the subject! So what's up? How have you been?"

"Oh, Lizzie," Megan signed, "it gets so boring sometimes! Do you ever feel like you're the only deaf kid in the world?"

"Not really," answered Lizzie. "I go to an all-deaf school! Almost everybody I know is deaf! Sometimes I feel like I'm the only one with a sense of humor—but there's *always* somebody deaf around!"

"Not at my school," said Megan. "I'm the only one."

"Bummer," said Lizzie. "Wow, I feel really bad for you." She tossed her blond hair back over her shoulders, acting like a mean girl in high school, pretending to care more than she actually did.

"My mom thought you could relate," said Megan, "but I guess she was wrong." She sulked slightly—and pouted and sighed.

"Hey, okay, what's the matter?" asked Lizzie, with real concern. "What happened?"

"Same old thing that happens all the time," Megan groused. "The deaf girl asks a stupid question and all the nondeaf kids get to laugh. 'Look at Megan; she's so funny!'"

"Ouch," said Lizzie. "I'd hate that."

"I do hate it," said Megan. "Sometimes I get angry and sometimes I cry and sometimes I come home and eat a bowl of ice cream."

"Easy on the ice cream," said Lizzie. "You don't want to do that all the time."

"Did I say 'all the time'?" asked Megan. "No," she continued, answering her own question. "I only do it when I'm feeling really lonely and alone."

Lizzie understood completely. She pulled a sad face and drew tears on her cheeks to offer some comfort and support.

Megan offered a shy smile and rolled her eyes. *"Sorry,"* Megan continued, "I know I must sound all sorry for myself."

"No, I understand," said Lizzie. "You feel all alone! I've felt that way. When I was little, before I went to the all-deaf school, I even made up this friend for myself named Sparkle."

"Sparkle?" Megan repeated the word and made a gesture like twinkling stars in case she hadn't understood Lizzie correctly.

"I know!" Lizzie replied. "*Stupid* name. It's pretty embarrassing now but I was only seven when I made her up. I wonder whatever happened to her."

"So who was she?" asked Megan. "Some make-believe friend?"

"Yeah, you know, *imaginary*," Lizzie continued. "Sparkle was this fairy—okay, I really was seven. And I was the only one who could see her—which was great because Sparkle would fly around the house and spy on people and hear things and then tell me in sign language everything she heard everybody say!"

"You're kidding me!" said Megan.

"I know," said Lizzie. "Pretty funny, huh? Sparkle was a real *snoop*."

Megan snickered at the notion of Lizzie's imaginary fairy friend who hovered over the household eavesdropping on hearing people and reporting what they said. "So what'd you find out?" she asked. "What did Sparkle tell you?"

"She knew all about my brother's girlfriends," Lizzie bragged. "Like who said what to who—back and forth—before they kissed."

Megan cracked up at the idea of kissing while being spied on by a fairy. And the sight of Megan laughing so hard made

Lizzie crack up too. "You should get a fairy to spy on Matt," Lizzie urged. "They're really good at it."

"Oh, my brother, Matt, doesn't have girl-friends," Megan protested.

"He will," said Lizzie. "Trust me; he will."

"So what else did Sparkle say?"

"You know," Lizzie continued, "the usual mischievous fairy stuff. Like if I was upset with my mom or my dad, Sparkle would always tell me everything I should have said instead of what I actually said."

"I need a fairy like that," said Megan.

"We all do," said Lizzie.

"And where did Sparkle live?"

"I kept her in the closet," said Lizzie, jerking a thumb at the closet door behind her, "so she was always close by."

"And so what happened to Sparkle?" asked Megan.

"I don't know! I grew up!" Lizzie said, pretending to be a brat about it. "I got rid of Sparkle! She got fired!"

The girls laughed at the notion of firing a fairy.

Lizzie suddenly looked spooked and mysterious. She tossed a tentative glance over her shoulder at the closet door. "Unless you think maybe she's still in there!" she said, trembling with fear.

Both girls cracked up all over again.

"She probably sleeps in your shoe!" said Megan.

"I bet she chews holes in my sweaters!" said Lizzie.

By this point, Lizzie and Megan were laughing so hard that they were giddy. The giggles only got worse when they realized how much they were giggling already, and Megan found herself wiping tears from her eyes. She had been laughing so much that what she said next took her completely by surprise. "Oh, Lizzie, I wish you lived here," said Megan.

Lizzie smiled for a moment. "Me too," she signed. "Me too." They sat smiling at each other for a little while, not saying or signing anything. Then Lizzie added, "That way, maybe me and Sparkle could hide in your closet, sleep in your shoes, and chew on your sweaters!"

THREE
SOLO, IT IS

Megan and her brother, Matt, had developed a diplomatic method of eating peanut butter on crackers after their mother had told them to stop fighting over food while they watched television in the den.

This was the system: 1) Matt held the box of crackers while Megan held the jar of peanut butter and a butter knife; 2) Matt handed two crackers to Megan; 3) Megan spread a dab of peanut butter on one side of both crackers; 4) Megan handed one cracker back to Matt; 5) Matt and Megan chomped down on the crackers at the exact same time; and 6) they chewed.

The system worked really well. Matt and Megan could sprawl across the sofa for hours without bickering, quietly passing crackers back and forth, and chomping and chewing.

So Megan was surprised when Matt interrupted the cracker process by flapping his arms and shouting, "Hey, hey, hey!"

"Hey—what?" asked Megan.

"It's *Dad*," said Matt. He tugged on his ear to indicate the sound of their father coming through the door, and Matt briskly signed the words "Dad's home."

Megan got up from the couch, kept her focus on the television program, and held her arms open in the archway, expecting a quick hug from her father as he moved down the front hall toward the kitchen to say hello to her mother.

"No, no," Matt signed. "He doesn't want a hug from you. He wants you to *help* him. He said, *'Megan, come help me!'*"

Megan was irked. "Dad did not say that!" she balked. "Dad knows I'm *deaf*! He doesn't call out for me when he knows I can't hear!"

"Well, you're up already," Matt continued, waving lazily from the sofa, "so go help him." And then he *laughed*.

Megan gasped. Sometimes she could not

believe how sneaky her brother was. She swatted his sneaker that was hanging off the edge of the sofa. "You go help him," she said. "I'm watching television."

Matt leaned back on the sofa and hollered, "Daaaa-aaad!" Megan caught a bit of the pitch—and from the way Matt was projecting, Megan could tell that he was being really loud. "Daaa-aad, Megan's coming!" he yelled. "She said she wants to help!"

Megan threw her hands on her hips. "No, I'm not!" she shouted back. "Matt's coming!"

"Megan is!" Matt shouted.

"Matt is!" Megan retorted, throwing herself onto the sofa and grabbing a pillow in protest.

At that same moment, Lainee headed down the hall, drying her wet hands on a dish towel half-tossed over her shoulder. "Your father called from the car to say he was coming home with a *surprise*," she said, "but he wouldn't tell me what it is." She stopped at the den and poked her head through the archway to add, "If you bums don't get off the sofa, you're going to miss your father's *big surprise* in the front yard."

Megan and Matt exchanged a quick

look—and then, in an instant, they both raced through the archway. Megan took the corner faster and ducked past her mother in the hall.

"Hey, no fair!" Matt protested, stuck behind his mother in the corridor. "Roadblock! Roadblock!"

"Please don't refer to me as a road-block," said Lainee. "I am your *mother*."

Down the hall, Megan laughed as she seized the doorknob and flung open the door. All she could see was her father tossing a white ball across the front lawn.

That's it? thought Megan. *A white ball? What kind of surprise is a lousy white ball?*

Suddenly, a large furry black-and-white dog leaped out of nowhere and snatched the ball in midair. "Good boy!" said her dad, as the dog trotted across the lawn and dropped the ball at his feet. By this point, Lainee and Matt were standing beside Megan. All three of them gaped at the dog, that was standing on the lawn as though he owned it.

"The surprise is a *dog*?" said Megan. She watched as the dog snatched the ball back with its mouth.

"A *big* dog," said Lainee, not entirely pleased.

"He's not that big," said David. "He just looks big because he's so lively."

"Cool!" said Matt, heading onto the grass to rub the dog's head with both hands. "Toss me the ball, Dad!"

Megan's dad, David, pried the ball from the dog's jaw, chucked it toward Matt, and shook his hand afterward to get rid of the dog's slobber. David walked toward Lainee at the front of the house, reaching to tug the kitchen towel from her shoulder and wipe his hand clean.

"Not on my fresh kitchen towel," said Lainee, retreating on the front porch. "Go get a rag."

"What's the matter?" said David. "You don't like the dog?"

Lainee looked mystified. "Dog? What dog?" she asked. She looked up, down, and sideways as though she didn't see a dog anywhere. "This is the first time I've heard anything about a dog. Have we ever discussed bringing a new dog into the family? No, we couldn't have—because you certainly would have talked about it with me first, right?"

Megan joined Matt and the dog in the yard. The dog darted excitedly about the grass, in constant motion, smelling everything he could and generally claiming the territory. At some point, the dog stopped in his tracks, not a foot away from Megan. He turned to look at her. Megan looked back.

"It's okay, puppy," she said. "I won't bite." She lowered into a squat and held out her hand. The dog extended his neck and nudged his nose gingerly toward Megan's hand, looking at her with big brown eyes that seemed to say, "You can pet me if you want."

Megan scratched his chin and then let her hand travel until she was scratching more vigorously behind the dog's ears. The dog let out a happy bark. He panted rapidly, letting his tongue drop out of his mouth, almost as though he was laughing.

Wow, thought Megan. *We have a dog again!*

Only months before, Megan and her family had had to put their dog, Apples, to sleep when he got too old and tired. Apples had a scruffy face and shaggy whiskers that made him look like a little old man. That made sense in a way because Apples was thirteen years old, which is really old for a dog. But this dog—laughing, barking, and charging about the yard—wasn't like a little old man at all. This dog was like some kind of wild boy.

"Where did he come from?" Lainee asked David on the front porch. "How did he get here? Who's going to feed him? Who's going to walk him? Who's going to give him a bath? Who said we wanted another dog in the first place?"

"Remember Ron at work?" David asked Lainee. "The bald guy in Accounting?"

Lainee shrugged. "No, I don't."

"Well, Ron and his wife found this dog in the parking lot at the mall. No collar, no tags—but he seemed like a sweet dog. So they took him to the vet to get him checked out. Everything checked out fine. But when they got him home, he turned out to be too much dog for their apartment—"

"'Too much dog!' Oh boy!" Lainee interrupted. "So what did the dog do?"

"Just a few chewed-up pillows, nothing that bad," David continued. "But he was clearly too big for a one bedroom apartment. Ron thought the dog needed a bigger house with a big yard—"

"So Ron should buy a bigger house with

a big yard," said Lainee. "I'm not hearing any reason why this dog should live with us."

"I guess I've been talking to Ron about missing Apples," David admitted. "I miss having a dog."

"It's a little *soon* to replace Apples, don't you think?" asked Lainee. "And, besides, didn't you think to ask me? It didn't occur to you to discuss a new dog with your wife?"

"He still doesn't have a name yet," said David, sounding more and more like a little boy. "Ron and his wife called him Puppy but he's too big to call Puppy. I thought you could come up with a better name. You were always so good with names and all." He glanced toward their kids, who were playing with the dog.

"Mom!" Matt shouted from the yard. "Look how big his feet are!"

It was true. The dog had enormous feet.

"He's part German shepherd," said David. "They have big feet."

"Oh, great!" said Lainee. "Big muddy dog tracks all across my house."

"Part German shepherd and part Border collie," David explained. "That's why he's black and white with a big fuzzy tail. And the combination makes a much smarter dog."

"I'm not sold," said Lainee.

Megan wrapped her arms around the dog's neck. The dog responded by licking her face three or four times. "See how smart he is?" said Megan. "He's so smart he already knows I'm beautiful! He can't stop licking me!"

"He's not kissing your beauty, Godzilla," said Matt. "He's licking the peanut butter off your face."

"Can we keep him, Mom?" asked Megan, in spoken words and in sign. "Please?"

"Are we keeping him, Mom?" asked Matt, in sign language too.

"Honey—?" asked David, shrugging his shoulders sheepishly. "It's only a dog. It's not the end of the world. It's not like I came home with—*two* dogs."

The kids laughed as though it was a much funnier joke than it was. They could tell from the way their dad was acting that it was a good time to make their mother laugh.

Lainee didn't respond. She looked down and shook her head distractedly. "I know what's going to happen," she said. "I'm going to end up walking him. I'm going to end up bathing him."

"I'll walk him," said Matt. "I won't let you walk him."

"I bet he's not housebroken," said Lainee. "He'd better not mess up my house!"

"Never, Mom, never," Matt assured her. "I'll walk him five times a day!"

"And I'll bathe him," said Megan. "He can take a bath with me. We'll take our baths together!"

Lainee's eyes widened with alarm as she tried to picture her daughter sharing the bathtub with a dog. "It's okay!" said David, patting her back. "Megan and I will scrub him down and hose him off in the backyard."

"I don't want him on the furniture, and he's not allowed to beg for food at the dinner table," Lainee continued. "The living room is off limits as well. And he needs a flea collar and a leash and a bowl and—"

"Mom!" Megan protested. "I love you, you know I love you—but enough with the rules! Is it yes or no? Can we keep the dog?"

"Okay!" said Lainee, tossing her hands. "Okay—yes! We can keep the dog. I want to say no but I'm outnumbered! Three to one!"

David, Megan, and Matt cheered. Even the dog joined in with a surprising bark. "I'm sorry," said Lainee. "Not three to one. It's four! I forgot to count the dog. I mean, Puppy. I mean—whatever-your-name-is."

David and Lainee exchanged a quick smile.

"So what do we name him?" said David.

"'Garth the Destroyer!'" said Matt. "That's a great name for a dog."

"Mom, no!" cried Megan, tugging on her mother's jeans.

"'Garth the Destroyer!'" Matt repeated. "It's a great name to me!"

"Dad!" Megan pleaded.

"We are not going to name him Garth the Destroyer," declared her father. "That's a name for a comic book. That is no name for a dog."

"Thank you, David," said Lainee, gazing down at Megan, still with her arm wrapped around the dog's neck. "So what would you like to name the dog, Megan?"

"I was thinking something like—Solo," Megan said.

"Solo?" Matt repeated with scorn.

"How did you come up with a name like Solo?" asked her father.

"It means 'all by yourself,'" Megan explained. "And Solo was 'all by himself' before he found us. And he found his way here 'all by himself.'"

"I don't care," said Matt dismissively. "Solo is not a good name for a dog either. It needs to be something you can shout across the neighborhood. You can't shout 'Solo!' and be heard down the street. Watch!"

He cupped his hands and tilted his head back for a Tarzan yell—except what he hollered was "Solo!"

It rang down the street loud and clear.

"What do you know?" Matt admitted with some surprise. "That was actually pretty good."

"Sounded good to me," said David.

Solo lifted his head and barked twice in agreement. The whole family laughed.

"Solo likes it," said Megan.

"I guess we're agreed," said David. "'Solo' it is."

FOUR
WIZARD

How many people . . . ?" Ms. Endee announced as she wrote at the whiteboard.

Megan couldn't read her teacher's lips when she faced the board but she could see Jann beside the teacher's desk. Jann translated the beginning of Ms. Endee's question, drawing a quick question mark and wiggling her fingers to indicate "people." The quizzical expression on Jann's face let Megan know there was more to come.

"How many people have seen the movie . . . ?" Ms. Endee continued, still writing. Jann added the translation for "have seen the movie." The sign for "movie" was based on an old-fashioned film projector, shaking one hand with fingers outstretched to suggest the flicker of light.

Ms. Endee stepped aside from what she had written on the board and completed her question "How many people have seen the movie . . . ?" By this point, every kid in class could read the writing on the board. Ms. Endee had written the words "The Wizard of Oz."

Every hand in the room shot into the air. Even students who never volunteered in class wanted to be recognized for having seen *The Wizard of Oz*.

"We have it on videotape," said Randy Vera.

"We own the DVD," said Cindy.

"I've only watched it a hundred billion gazillion times," said Ronnie Jiu. Without anyone requesting it, he launched into his imitation of the Cowardly Lion. Naturally, all the kids laughed.

"Okay, okay," said Ms. Endee. "Settle down." She gestured for the students to lower their hands but many didn't. If Ms. Endee was handing out DVD copies of *The Wizard of Oz*, they didn't want to miss the chance for a freebie.

"Now, tell me," the teacher continued,

"how many people know that *The Wizard of Oz* was first a *book*?"

Almost every hand fell back onto its desk with a thump. The only hand still raised belonged to Alexis Powell, the smart girl who sat in the back of the classroom near Megan.

"Alexis?"

"Yes, *The Wizard of Oz* was a book before it was a movie," Alexis declared, which was a pretty obvious statement under the circumstances. Alexis had transferred to Wilmot Elementary School from a private school in the fall, and she was still in the habit of keeping her hand in the air even after she'd been called on to answer. Sometimes when Megan imitated Alexis behind her back, she kept one hand raised in the air.

"Yes, but have you read it?" Ms. Endee asked. "The book?"

"Not exactly," said Alexis, finally lowering her hand. "I know it's a book, but I haven't actually read it."

"Well, today's your lucky day," said Ms. Endee, "because look what I have." She opened a large cardboard box on top of her desk and tilted it forward so that everyone could see. The box contained several copies of the same single book. "*The Wonderful Wizard of Oz*," Ms. Endee announced, "by L. Frank Baum."

A low murmur of excitement swept over the classroom.

"We each get a copy?" asked Cindy.

"Plenty for everyone," said Ms. Endee.

"And do we have to read it?" asked Ronnie Jiu.

"Not only read it," said Ms. Endee, "but you're going to *stage* it."

As if on cue, a lady stepped into the door frame. She was somewhat heavyset with a thick mane of curly brown hair, a big toothy smile and large, rather thick eyeglasses. She wore a flowing dress with a bright floral pattern on it. "Hello!" the woman declared, as though the classroom had been expecting her arrival.

"Class, I'd like you to meet Ms. Ceil Scherer," said Ms. Endee. "She will be leading our drama component this spring."

Drama? thought Megan. But before she could raise her hand to ask a question, Ms. Scherer launched into her address.

"Let me introduce myself," she began. "I'm an actress and a director, and I work with several small theaters in the area. Can anybody tell me the difference between theater and—say, television or the movies?"

The class waited for Alexis to raise her hand and answer. Sure enough, Ms. Scherer acknowledged Alexis's hand.

"The theater is *live*?" said Alexis, raising her inflection slightly at the end of the sentence so that it sounded more like a question.

"Well, yes, that's it precisely," said Ms. Scherer. "The theater is live. When you watch television or a movie, the actors don't know you're watching them. But when you see a play in the theater, the audience and the performers are both—*alive*—and the play is happening right here, right now." She breezed to the front of the classroom and scooped a copy of *The Wonderful Wizard of Oz* off Ms. Endee's desk to hold it aloft. "And what we're going to do is to turn *The Wonderful Wizard of Oz* into a play for the whole school," she announced.

A louder wave of excitement swept across the room.

"We're doing the movie?" cried Casey Waite. "I love that movie!" But before she could break into a chorus of her favorite song, her teacher stopped her.

"*No*, Casey," Ms. Endee said emphatically. She moved up and down the aisles, distributing one copy of the book to each individual student. "We are *not* doing the movie. We are doing the book!"

"Here's my idea," said Ms. Scherer, taking charge. "What I want you to do is to read the book and come up with your *own* way to tell the original story—as a *play*. Then we can assign roles and I'll write some scenes for you to perform and we'll put the show together. But you have to read the book first. And you can't cheat and simply watch the movie again instead because the story in the book is quite a bit different."

"Are there Flying Monkeys in the book?" asked Brian Murphy.

"Yes, there are," said Ms. Scherer.

"Good," said Brian Murphy, "because the Flying Monkeys are my favorite part."

"What about witches?" asked Megan. "Are there good witches and bad witches?"

Jann translated Megan's question, and Ms. Scherer answered it. "Yes," she said, "and there's Dorothy and her little dog, Toto, too . . ."

The class tittered with excitement.

". . . and the Cowardly Lion and the Scarecrow and the Tin Woodman," Ms. Scherer continued.

"But a lot of stuff in the book never made it to the movie," interjected Ms. Endee, "and I expect you to notice the differences."

Alexis raised her hand.

"Yes, Alexis," said Ms. Endee.

"How do we put the book on the stage?" she asked.

Ms. Endee turned to the drama teacher. "That's the big trick," said Ms. Scherer. "It's a *lot* of work. We figure out which scenes to include and how to stage them. And we figure out—"

"—what songs to sing?" interrupted Ronnie Jiu.

"We're making our *own* version of *The Wizard of Oz*," said Ms. Scherer. "So we can't use the songs from the movie because those songs belong to the movie. They don't belong to us."

"So what songs do we sing?" asked Megan.

"What songs do you know?" said Ms. Scherer. "What songs do you like?"

"You mean like—any songs at all?" said Ronnie. "Like—'I've Been Working on the Railroad'?" All the children laughed.

"Why not?" asked Ms. Scherer. "I think that would be funny, don't you? All the Flying Monkeys singing about the Wicked Witch. 'I've Been Working on the Railroad!'"

The entire classroom laughed—as much to hear Ms. Scherer sing as to imagine the Flying Monkeys singing.

"But that would be wrong," said Alexis, "because it doesn't make sense."

"We'll find songs that make sense," said Ms. Scherer.

"And in the movie," said Casey, "the Flying Monkeys don't *sing*."

"But they could," Ms. Scherer insisted. "We're staging the book—not the movie— and the book came first. We can stage the story any way we want to."

"And who's going to be in it?" asked Cindy.

"You are," said Ms. Scherer. "We'll hold auditions next week but I don't want you to freak out and get all nervous and everything. I just want to see how you handle yourself onstage."

"What do you want us to get onstage and *do*?" asked Ronnie.

"Anything you want," said Ms. Scherer. "Prepare a special skill, if you've got one. Juggle, do a cartwheel, or recite a poem. Sing a song or two if you can, but you don't have to. We're looking for a Dorothy, a Scarecrow, a Cowardly Lion, and a Tin Woodman who can sing—so if you want to play any of those roles, let us hear you sing."

The class chattered excitedly at the prospect of actually singing in front of one another. Ms. Endee clapped her hands loudly three times to get them to quiet down. Then she announced that rehearsals were scheduled for three days a week, Tuesday, Wednesday, and Thursday, for an hour and a half after school, from 3:30 until 5:00—over the course of eight weeks.

"Two months?!" cried Ronnie Jiu.

"It's not a lot of time—considering the amount of work we have to do," said Ms. Scherer. "So if you're not up to the commitment, please be sure to let us know now."

Cindy's hand was raised. "What if you don't want to be in the show?" she asked. "I mean, *I* do. But I know some people are shy. Maybe they don't want to participate."

"You don't have to be *in* the show," said Ms. Scherer, "but everybody has to participate. It's your show, people, not mine. You're the ones who are going to write it and design it and perform it."

The class was silent for a moment. The task seemed too huge. "But we don't know how to do that," said Megan simply.

Ms. Endee stepped forward. "I don't know how many times I have to remind you guys," she said, "but this is a school. You're not going to get out of here without learning something. You didn't know how to stage a book when you came in here this morning; that's what you're going to do before the end of the year."

Naturally, *The Wonderful Wizard of Oz* dominated the lunchtime conversation. Everyone was preoccupied trying to imagine who should play what and how to stage a tornado, build Emerald City, make a witch melt—and make a monkey fly.

"I think the Emerald City should be purple," said Megan.

"It can't be," said Cindy. "Emeralds are green."

"So we make it the Sapphire City," argued Megan. "Some sapphires are purple."

"If you make it the Sapphire City," said Cindy, "nobody's going to recognize it's *The Wizard of Oz*."

"As long as we have Dorothy, the Scarecrow, the Tin Woodman, and the Cowardly Lion," said Megan, "we could send them to the moon, and people would know it's *The Wizard of Oz*."

"But I don't want to do the moon version," said Alexis. "I want to do the real thing."

"Me too," said Cindy.

"I'm just saying ours could be different," said Megan. "The real thing is only what we make it."

"Whatever," said Bethany. "I'm just so excited we're doing *The Wizard of Oz*!"

"It's a dream," said Cindy.

"It's not actually a dream," said Alexis.

"I know that," said Cindy. "I only mean—pinch me, I'm dreaming. I'm that excited."

"I meant in the book," Alexis continued. "It's not a dream in the book. I took a peek at the first chapter, and the story is not a dream. In the movie, it's a dream—"

"I remember," said Megan, "'and you were there and you were there and you were there too.'" She pointed at Cindy, Alexis, and Bethany.

"—but in the book, it really happens," Alexis continued. "Dorothy really goes to a land called Oz."

"Weird," said Bethany.

"I think it's a trick," Cindy announced in a brash declaration. "Ms. Endee is trying to trick us into reading another book!"

"I don't care about any of that," said Megan. "All I know is that one was the book, and the other was the movie—but this will be a play that we all get to be in!" She threw her hands in the air and added, laughing, "We get to be the Leading Ladies!" All the girls laughed and began bowing and blowing kisses to one another like big important actresses. Megan threw herself across the table to autograph Bethany's notebook.

"Except we don't know what parts we're playing yet," said Cindy. "Ms. Endee and Ms. Scherer have to decide. We could all end up being Munchkins."

"I'm not being a Munchkin," said Megan.

"You could!" said Cindy.

"Ms. Endee would not make us all play Munchkins," Megan argued. "Or Ms. Scherer, either!"

"She sure could!" Cindy insisted. "She gets to decide who plays what, depending on how well we do at the audition."

Megan was quiet.

"When are the auditions?" said Alexis.

"Ms. Scherer posted a sign saying next Wednesday," said Bethany. "That way we can work on our auditions over the weekend."

Megan was still quiet.

"You mean I have to spend the weekend figuring out what I'm going to do for my audition?" Alexis asked.

"You'd better if you don't want to be a Munchkin," said Cindy. Alexis, Bethany, and Cindy laughed but Megan was still quiet.

"Oh," added Bethany, mostly to break the silence. "And we're not calling it *The Wizard of Oz*—even though the story is going to be the same. Ms. Scherer says we're going to call it '*Wizard!*'"

"Oh, I like that," said Alexis.

"I wonder who's going to play the wizard!" said Cindy.

"Well, I'm not going to worry about it," said Megan, finally speaking again. "Ms. Scherer has to give us all great parts! She simply has to! We're the Leading Ladies!"

The girls cheered and laughed again.

At that moment, Tony Rosenblum barged into the group at their table. "I'll trade my carrot sticks for anything sweet," he said.

"Tony, do you think we're really putting on a show?" asked Alexis.

"We're putting on a show, all right," Tony replied. "I overheard Ms. Endee ask Principal Smelter if he would get the piano in the auditorium tuned."

The girls ogled one another with widened eyes. "I guess this is going to happen," said Alexis.

"No skin off my nose whether it happens or not," said Tony with a dismissive sniff. "I'm not getting onstage in front of all those people."

"But you have to," said Megan. "Ms. Endee said everyone has to be in the play."

"I don't have to do anything I don't want to," said Tony. "My dad says I'm 'slow to warm.'"

"What does that mean?" asked Megan.

"I think I'm shy or something," said Tony.

"You don't seem so shy to me," said Megan.

"Tell my dad," Tony Rosenblum replied as he pushed away from the table.

"What's the point of being shy?" said Megan.

"I'm shy!" Alexis announced. "But I'm happy to be in the play as long as I don't play anything big. I'm happy with a small role."

"Are you a good witch—or a bad witch?" said Megan, imitating the good witch in the movie.

"I'm probably going to end up being one of those angry trees," said Alexis. "Anything that's tall."

"Me too," said Casey. Alexis and Casey were the tallest girls in class.

"Then maybe you should both practice throwing apples," said Bethany. "Is that in the book? The part about throwing apples?"

"Haven't gotten that far yet," Alexis said with a shrug.

"I've decided what I want to be in the play," Cindy declared, "and here's a list." She pulled out her notebook and read a list that she had scribbled down the margin of one page, around the bottom, and up the margin on the opposite side. "Auntie Em, the Scarecrow, the Tin Woodman, or the Good Witch of the North. Not the Wicked Witch, even though that would probably be a lot of fun. I don't know—maybe the Wicked Witch wouldn't be so bad."

"I don't really see you as the bad witch type," said Megan.

"No?" asked Cindy. "Maybe not. Okay, I wouldn't mind being the Cowardly Lion but I probably won't get it because I'm not that funny. I don't want to be a Munchkin unless I'm like the Mayor's wife or something. I'm okay being anybody in the Emerald City. But if I get cast as a Flying Monkey, I'm telling you right now, I'm probably going to cry, and I won't come to any of the rehearsals so you can just practice the play without me."

The whole table laughed.

"Who do you want to be in the play, Megan?" asked Alexis.

"I don't know," said Megan. "Something good."

"I wonder who's going to get cast as Dorothy," said Bethany.

Megan almost piped up to say that she'd

play Dorothy if nobody else wanted the part—but before she did, Cindy spoke up again.

"I think Casey should play the Tin Woodman," she declared, "because Casey is tall, she wears braces, and she can stand on her head." It was a suggestion that made sense and made no sense at all—so the girls all had to argue about that for a while, and Megan missed her chance to say anything about wanting to play Dorothy.

Ms. Endee passed among the cafeteria tables, clapping her hands to call the students back to order. "Line up in five minutes," she said.

"Ms. Endee, Ms. Endee," said Cindy, waving her hand to attract her teacher's attention.

"What is it, Cindy?" Ms. Endee replied.

"Isn't it true that you and Ms. Scherer get to decide who plays what in *The Wizard of Oz*?"

"I suppose it is," said Ms. Endee, "although it's mostly Ms. Scherer's responsibility. And I'm sure Jann will probably help us. It all depends on those auditions next week."

"Yes, Ms. Endee," the table replied.

"Four minutes till lineup," Ms. Endee added, before moving on to other tables.

The girls gathered their trays and crossed the cafeteria to empty them into the garbage. Megan tugged on Cindy's sleeve to keep her behind the other girls.

"What's the big deal?" asked Cindy.

"I have to ask," said Megan. "Who do you think is going to be Dorothy?"

"Oh, I don't know!" Cindy replied. "I guess it all depends on the auditions. But one thing's for sure—" She held the hinged lid on the trash receptacle so Megan could empty her tray.

"What's that?" asked Megan, tossing her milk carton into the bin.

"Competition is going to be *fierce*!" Cindy released the lid so that it thwacked back and forth—and signed five or six exclamation points, right in Megan's face.

FIVE
MIRROR, MIRROR

Megan had a secret that no one knew.

Every now and then—well, actually, a lot more often than that—Megan locked herself in the upstairs bathroom. She pushed a foot stool in front of the sink and stood at the bathroom mirror. There, gazing at her own reflection, Megan pretended to be all sorts of people—*instead of herself.*

That afternoon, for example, Megan was a doctor, a nurse, a little orphan boy with a broken arm, an airplane pilot, a flight attendant, *and* a nun in the gripping tale of an ill-fated missionary flight over a vast, uncharted South American jungle. The flight attendant, a pretty girl named

Jill, had just informed the passengers that the plane was going to crash. Megan placed her feet together in the center of the stool and held her shoulders back, her hands at her sides, so that Jill stood with quiet authority.

"In case of an emergency, like the one we're in right now," Jill politely explained, "everyone will be provided with life jackets and oxygen masks."

Naturally, the passengers freaked out.

"Doctor Bob is having a heart attack!" cried Nurse Betty, climbing over her chair and waving a box of cotton balls. "Does anybody know CPR?"

"Don't you know CPR?" asked Sergio, the little orphan boy from Guatemala. His broken arm was wrapped in a gauze bandage, and his voice was slightly muffled inside the oxygen mask.

"I did, but I forgot," explained Nurse Betty—and unfortunately, Doctor Bob was turning bright blue in the bathroom mirror.

"Everybody, brace yourself!" cried Flight Attendant Jill. "This plane is going to crash!"

At this point, even Sister Ursula set aside her prayer book and began to scream. A large white bath towel came in handy for Megan's quick costume change into Sister Ursula.

"What are you *doing*?" asked Matt.

Megan jumped at the sight of her brother in the bathroom mirror, staring at her from the open doorway behind her. "Privacy, *please*, you freak!" she said in an indignant snit, realizing she had forgotten to lock the door.

"I need to use the bathroom," Matt urged.

"Go downstairs!" shouted Megan, still in a frenzy.

Matt didn't budge. "Yeah, sure," he said vaguely, "but—what are you *doing*?"

When Matt had opened the door, Sister Ursula had been clutching her veil and shrieking wildly as the plane pitched back and forth, clipping the dense jungle below. Megan still had the white bath towel thrown over her head.

"I'm drying my hair!" Megan said to her brother. "Do you mind?"

"Yeah, so okay," Matt replied, "but— why are you *screaming*?"

"I've got tangles!" shouted Megan, kicking the door shut with her foot.

*

Once the door was safely shut, Sister Ursula jumped to safety from the back of the descending airplane and landed among the leafy treetops. In the same motion, Megan lunged to lock the bathroom door—and to double-check the lock so that she wouldn't be interrupted again.

Megan couldn't believe she had forgotten to lock the bathroom door. It wasn't like her to overlook something like that. In the past, she had hogged the bathroom for hours, play-acting in the mirror—and pretending to be more deaf than she actually was when Matt had pounded on the door. The only reason she could possibly have forgotten the lock today was because she was so distracted by all the excitement over the auditions for *The Wizard of Oz* next week.

Even before Megan's hand released the doorknob, she found that her imagination had already taken a turn into another story. She was no longer on an airplane—or even in the jungle. In fact, she was no longer *human*.

Megan had turned into Sparkle, a mischievous fairy who lived among the forgotten shoes in the closet of a certain deaf girl whose big brother insisted on kissing all the wrong potential girlfriends. Sparkle wiggled through the keyhole to spy on the foolish brother. Hopefully, she could stop him before he proposed marriage to the evil, ugly, wicked bachelorette. Sparkle hovered among the shower curtains and, once the coast was clear, she darted across the bathroom and landed on the edge of the sink.

Megan shook off the fairy and stared at herself in the bathroom mirror. She didn't really know where the Sparkle story was going and, besides, she was tired of hooking her thumbs in her armpits and twitching her elbows to imitate little buzzing wings.

"What am I doing for *this audition*?" she asked herself in the mirror. She waited briefly for a response—but since the mirror wasn't magic, nothing came back.

When Megan had asked, Jann had explained that Ms. Scherer wanted students to "sing a short song and then a different short song—like one happy, one sad."

"And if you don't want to sing," Jann had continued, "Ms. Scherer said to come in with some special skill. Like some little trick that you can do."

It sounded as if Megan was going to have to do a solo in front of the class after all. But what could she do? She had already been laughed at once about a "solo." She didn't want it to happen again.

"What 'special skills' do *I* have?" Megan signed to herself in the mirror. "And how am I supposed to sing a song? I'm not a singer!"

"Has anybody seen Megan?" asked her father downstairs.

"She's upstairs in the bathroom," said Matt.

"She promised to help me wash the dog," said David.

"She's upstairs," Matt repeated.

"Would you go get her for me?" said David.

"I already walked in on her once, Dad," said Matt. "Trust me, she doesn't want to be disturbed in the bathroom."

"Well, she'll be down soon, I suppose."

"I wouldn't count on it, Dad," said Matt. "If you need to use the bathroom, you'd better go downstairs."

"It's not that," said David. "I want to make sure your mom sees us washing the dog. Do you want to help?"

"Hey, I signed up to walk the dog," Matt replied. "I didn't sign up to wash him. That's Megan's department."

"You're right," said David. "And if she's doing that thing in the mirror, she'll be up there forever."

At that same moment, back in the bathroom, Megan filled the sink with water and splashed the surface with both hands. She had taken on the role of Niagara, a mermaid who lived on a rock in a faraway sea. Niagara splashed her tail in the water while she sang to lure the sailors whose ships always crashed into the rocks. It was terribly sad but terribly exciting.

"Megan is still in the bathroom," David said to Lainee, when he found her in the backyard garden.

"Is she?" said Lainee, on her knees in front of a flower bed.

"Yeah, I didn't clock when she went in," said David, "but it's been a little while."

"She'll come out eventually," said Lainee, continuing to dig.

"What does she do in there?" asked David.

"I don't see her wearing makeup, if

that's what you're upset about."

"Not really," said Megan's dad.

"Then I wouldn't worry," said Lainee. "Young girls like their 'alone-time.'" She set aside her garden trowel and brushed the dirt off her gardening gloves.

"You don't think she's doing that thing in the mirror?" asked David.

"What thing?" asked Lainee.

"*You know*," said David, "that crazy thing when she tells herself stories and plays all the characters in the bathroom mirror."

"Oh, I don't think she does that anymore," said Lainee.

"You don't?"

"No," said Lainee. "Megan stopped doing that a long time ago."

"Really?" said David. "What about the time we had to call the fire department to take the door off the hinges 'cause she'd been in there so long and wouldn't answer and we were afraid what might have happened?"

"David," said Lainee, turning back to her petunias, "that was two years ago, at least."

"Really?" asked Megan's dad, scratching his head. "I could swear it was last week."

*

Niagara's favorite mermaid song was "Let There Be Peace on Earth"—which also happened to be a song that Megan had learned at summer camp with Cindy and Lizzie. It was the perfect song for Niagara because the words were so beautiful and the music was so sweet.

When Niagara saw a ship on the horizon, she pulled out all the stops with "Let There Be Peace on Earth." Since Megan had already worked on the movements to the words at summer camp, Niagara was able to give a terrific polished performance.

She wasn't actually singing the melody, of course. Megan understood about music and melody but since she couldn't actually hear melody, she didn't risk trying to sing it. Instead, her hands told the story, fluttering like butterflies from one image to the next. Her body swayed more or less in rhythm to the music and her face added all the emotions, from joy to sadness to courage. The effect was quite remarkable. As Niagara, Megan was as-good-as singing, dancing, and telling a story—all at the same time.

Naturally, the sailors went wild.

*

David found Matt in the den in front of the television. "Will you watch the dog for me?" he asked.

"No fair, Dad!" Matt protested. "I shouldn't have to wash him! I already walked him. Megan's supposed to wash him."

"All right already," said David. "I didn't say, 'Wash the dog.' I said, 'watch' him. I'm going to get Megan out of the bathroom— and I don't want your mother to find out how smelly the dog is today." He pulled a piece of paper out of a desk drawer and wrote on it in large black letters.

"How are you getting Megan out of the bathroom?" asked Matt, suddenly curious.

"It's a little trick I learned in law school," said David. "I'm making a written request."

Niagara the mermaid was surprised to see a rubber inner tube bobbing in the ocean among the rocks. It contained Captain Ricky, a seafaring explorer in search of a rare purple penguin.

"Perhaps you've seen this penguin," said Captain Ricky, putting aside the long-handled shower brush he was using as a paddle. "Instead of black and white, this particular penguin is purple and deep purple."

"Of course!" Niagara replied with a laugh. "Who could miss a purple penguin? That's my favorite color! He lives on an island over by the bathtub. We could share a ride on my turtle, if you like."

"Lead the way!" said Captain Ricky, as they perched together on the edge of the toilet.

In the credits that rolled across the bathroom mirror at the end of the Niagara story, Megan played the mermaid, the explorer, the penguin, and even the wise old turtle. Today, however, the story gained a new scene.

"Oh, Niagara, sing that song again," said Captain Ricky, as he and Niagara shared the rock with the penguin. "You sing so beautifully."

"But I'm not really singing," the mermaid replied. "What I do is different from singing."

"Do it again, whatever it is," said Captain Ricky. "It's so beautiful."

Megan stopped to look at herself in the bathroom mirror. The way she sang—as herself and as Niagara—*was* beautiful.

I'm singing as good as anyone else, she thought.

Megan used to get Matt to help her

learn all the words to Billy Joel songs, and she would sign them along with the music. When she had showed Cindy how she could sing and sign Billy Joel's "Just the Way You Are," Cindy had said that Megan's version was actually even *better* than singing. For a moment, Megan wondered whether she should sing another Billy Joel song for her audition, but she also wanted to sing something new.

On the spot, Megan decided to sing "Let There Be Peace on Earth" as her audition piece. For the different song, she thought she'd sing the "Pink Lady" song from camp—the one that she and the other girls in her cabin had made up—but then she thought it might not sound right for an audition. She decided to sing "She'll Be Coming Round the Mountain" instead. She and Lizzie had spent hours figuring out the gestures for all the words in that song, while Cindy bravely sang on and on and on.

"Let There Be Peace on Earth" and "Coming Round the Mountain." It would be the perfect audition.

Megan didn't happen to hear the knock at the door because Niagara was already singing an encore of "Let There Be Peace on Earth" at Captain Ricky's request. She did actually hear the second knock at the door but decided it was a good opportunity to pretend she was too deaf.

A moment later, a paper slid under the doorjamb. Niagara was delivering the best part of the song, singing it with all her heart, when she noticed the paper out of the corner of her eye.

"Look, Captain Ricky," she said. "A note in a bottle."

"Perhaps it's a friendly message," said Captain Ricky.

"Let's see," said Niagara.

Megan hopped off the stool to retrieve the piece of paper. Big black letters were written across the page. It read: "Please help wash the dog. Dad."

Megan took the note back to the bathroom mirror and showed it to Captain Ricky and Niagara.

"What is it?" said Captain Ricky.

"New words!" said Niagara.

Niagara thought for a moment, leaned back against the rock, and began to sing, "Please help wash the dog!"

SIX
THE TRICKY PART

"If I was a spy," Tony Rosenblum declared, "I would use sign language so I could talk to other spies without anybody knowing what I was saying."

Megan nudged Cindy and rolled her eyes as they leaned against the stone ledge that surrounded the school playground. For some reason, Tony Rosenblum had spent the entire recess marching back and forth in front of the two girls, talking about becoming a *spy*.

"Tony," said Megan, "no offense, but you would make a terrible spy."

"How come?" said Tony.

"Because a whole lot of people speak sign language," Megan continued, "and they would all know what you were saying."

"Sign language looks secret," said Cindy, "but once you know it, it's no secret."

"That's why you'd make a terrible spy," Megan concluded.

"But I thought I'd use it like a secret code," Tony enthused, shaking his hands as if he was speaking sign language when he wasn't actually saying anything at all.

"You're not listening," said Cindy. "Sign language isn't secret. Anyone can learn it!"

"Besides," said Megan, "sign language is only secret if you're not paying attention. Usually it's obvious."

"'Obvious?'" said Tony. "I don't get it. How is it 'obvious'?"

Megan pushed off the wall so that she and Tony stood toe-to-toe. She shook out her arms like a gunslinger, preparing to launch into her explanation as though she'd done this a thousand times before. "The whole trick to sign language is that it means exactly what it says," said Megan. "It's *not* like when a softball catcher wiggles a few fingers to signal the pitcher for a curveball, and it's *not* like when a gambler cheats at cards." She tugged on her ear and winked at Cindy—who smiled back because it was the same signal they used when they were cheating at Spades.

"Signals like that can be secret," said Megan, "but the whole point of sign language is to make yourself understood. Which is why everything means exactly what it already means."

"I'm sorry." Tony Rosenblum looked perplexed. "I still don't get it."

"He's just being difficult," said Cindy.

"I don't get it!" Tony protested.

"It's okay!" Megan insisted, waving Cindy to back off. She turned to Tony and said, "Tony, what does this mean?" She raised her arm and waved across the playground.

"'Hello,'" said Tony, "but it also means 'good-bye.'"

"'Hello' or 'good-bye,'" Megan replied, "but you're gonna know which because you're either coming or going, right?"

"I guess so," said Tony.

"Good!" said Megan. "You're doing great! And what about when people go like this?" She raised her hand to her ear like a telephone receiver.

"Call me," said Tony.

"And this—?" said Megan, clapping her

hands in front of her and shaking them, ready to catch a ball.

"Throw me the ball."

"Exactly," said Megan. "Sign language is obvious like that. It's not complicated."

"But that's everyday stuff," said Tony. "Give me a real sign-language example."

Megan flipped her hands to indicate that his request was absolutely no problem. "Hey, Cindy," she said, "what's this?" She clawed at her own face like she was scratching whiskers.

"A tiger," said Cindy. It was suddenly a pop quiz.

"And this?" Megan continued. She threw a hand in front of her nose, like an elephant tossing its trunk.

"An elephant," said Cindy with a smirk. This quiz was awfully easy.

"And these?" Megan squeezed puffy shapes just above her head, like she was pinching the passing pillow.

"Those are clouds," said Cindy.

"And how about this?" she asked, tracing a single finger in wispy trails away from her forehead.

"That's a dream," said Cindy.

"Excellent," said Megan. "Last one for

Tony." She picked up what appeared to be a hamburger and held it in front of her face, ready to bite. "What's this?" she asked, mumbling the words like she had a mouth full of food.

"A hamburger?" said Tony.

"See what I mean?" said Megan, dropping her hands and letting the burger hit the ground. "It's obvious."

"But those are just the names of things," said Tony. "What happens when you get to sentences and paragraphs and whole conversations?"

"Oh yeah, well," said Megan, "that's the tricky part."

Tony stepped back to consider Megan with a new appreciation. "You should talk in sign language for your audition," he said, "you know—for *The Wizard of Oz*. It could be your special skill."

"I speak sign language every day," said Megan. "It's not so special to me."

"So which part did you decide to try out for anyway?" asked Tony.

Megan and Cindy exchanged a quick glance. Megan had already confided in Cindy that she wanted to play Dorothy. The news had made Cindy squeal so loudly that even Megan had felt a tingle in her ear. She had yet, however, to spring the news on any of their friends.

"Should I tell him?" Megan asked Cindy.

"Go ahead," said Cindy.

"Go ahead and what?" declared Tony.

"Not that it's any of your business," Megan asserted, "but I want to be Dorothy."

After a slight pause, Tony responded, "Dorothy?" as if he hadn't heard her correctly.

"Dorothy, yes, Dorothy," said Megan.

"But Dorothy is the whole story," said Tony.

"It's the lead role, yeah," Megan replied. "That's what I want."

"But she's in every scene," said Tony.

"You think I don't know the story, Tony?" asked Megan. "Yes, she's in every scene! She's the whole story! That's why I want to play Dorothy!"

"Well," said Tony, "it sure is going to be interesting if you do."

"What's that supposed to mean?" asked Megan.

"It will be interesting," Tony continued, "to have a main character who you can't really understand."

"You understand everything Megan says," Cindy argued. It was true. Between the sign language and spoken speech, most of the kids in Megan's class had grown completely accustomed to the way she talked.

"Here, maybe," said Tony, "but this is a playground. Not a play."

"So who do you want to be, Tony?" Cindy snapped with a sneer. "The Mayor of Munchkinland?"

"Yeah, I do," said Tony, quite confident and relaxed about it. "How'd you guess?"

Megan waved her hands to indicate that she was "through" with this conversation. "I want to play Dorothy," she repeated with emphasis. "I want it. It's my *dream!*"

To prove her point, Megan didn't actually say the word "dream." Instead, she wiggled one finger away from her forehead.

"I think he likes you," said Cindy, after Tony finally wandered away.

"Tony doesn't like *me*," replied Megan. "You're the one he likes."

"You think so?"

Megan noticed that Cindy wasn't putting up much of an argument.

"But you're the one he was talking to," Cindy offered.

"Only because I'm different," said Megan. "You're the one he likes."

Megan changed the subject to tell Cindy all about Solo, the new family dog, but their conversation was interrupted by the arrival of Maya Ackerman. "Casey just told me and I had to come over and ask. It's not true, is it?"

"Is what not true?" asked Cindy.

"Casey says Megan wants to be Dorothy," said Maya.

"Who told her that?" asked Cindy.

"Tony Rosenblum," said Maya, quite matter of fact.

"Sure," said Megan. "I want to be Dorothy."

"Not that there's anything wrong with that," said Maya. "Kaitlyn thought Elizabeth should be Dorothy but Elizabeth thought Keisha should be Dorothy, and it's all up to Ms. Scherer anyway."

"That's right," said Megan. "It's up to Ms. Scherer."

Katherine Kail joined them, slightly winded and carrying a half-deflated volleyball. "Hey, Megan," she said. "I heard about Dorothy."

"Don't tell me," said Megan. "Tony Rosenblum."

"How'd you know?" said Katherine.

"He told everybody," said Megan.

"Some spy, he turned out to be," said Cindy. "Instead of a spy, Tony Rosenblum should be a newscaster."

"I don't care," said Megan. "It's no secret."

"Not that *I* care either," said Katherine. "It's just going to be kind of weird and all."

"How is it weird?" asked Megan.

"I only meant, like, *cool* and weird," said Katherine.

"Well, whatever," said Megan. "it hasn't happened yet so—whatever."

"Right, I know," Katherine repeated, "whatever."

And then Ronnie Jiu appeared. "Hey, Megan," he said, "I heard you want to play Dorothy."

"Yes, I do," said Megan. "What's it to you?"

"Cool," said Ronnie. "I want to play the Cowardly Lion. Wouldn't that be cool? You as Dorothy and me as the Cowardly Lion?"

"Fingers crossed," said Megan.

"Fingers and toes," said Ronnie. "Good luck!"

SEVEN
SIT, SOLO, SIT

Lainee Merrill had a famous lasagna. Maybe not *world* famous but famous enough with family and friends so that whenever Wilmot Elementary School threw a potluck, the moms and dads on the PTA always suggested that Lainee make "that famous lasagna" because they knew it would go fast. If Matt's softball team won the big game, the players always celebrated with a double-sized victory lasagna. Whenever Lainee's own family honored a birthday, an anniversary, or just a good report card, Lainee found herself hauling out the lasagna pan.

Even though Lainee wasn't so wild about the new dog, she decided that Solo's arrival was a special occasion that deserved a famous lasagna—even if she had already declared that the dog was not allowed to beg for food at the table. Lainee had decided to be a good sport about the dog. She even pulled out the shelf paper to make a "Welcome Home, Solo!" banner. She planned to hang it in the dining room as a surprise.

And he is a handsome dog, she admitted to herself as she watched Solo trot about the fenced-in backyard through her kitchen window.

Lainee was carefully working on the third layer of the lasagna when she heard a frantic scratching at the back door. *What the heck is that?* she wondered. It took a moment before she realized that it must be Solo. She quickly washed her hands and reached for the kitchen door.

"All right already, Solo," she said, tugging on the doorknob. "Come inside then."

But Solo didn't budge. He waited for Lainee to do—something.

"What's up with you?" asked Lainee. "Are you coming inside or not?"

Solo lowered his head and dropped a dead lizard from his jaws onto the doorstep. Then he sat on his haunches, fairly pleased with himself, and panted contentedly.

"Oh, no!" Lainee cried with disgust. She looked past the dog and observed that all her flower beds, the careful, even rows of petunias, lilacs, and daffodils that had stretched across the garden, had been thoroughly trampled. "Solo!" she snapped.

Apparently the dog sensed that he was in trouble. He backed up a couple paces, whimpered apologetically, and inched forward to nudge the dead lizard closer to Lainee's shoes.

The happy surprise of Lainee's famous lasagna and Solo's "Welcome Home" banner were unfortunately upstaged by the dead lizard.

"We have to do something about that dog," Lainee declared, as she served heaping spoonfuls of lasagna onto plates at the dinner table that evening.

"He's not 'that dog.' His name is Solo," said Megan.

"I know his name," said Lainee. "I've been hollering 'Solo!' all day. '*Solo*, no!' '*Solo*, get down!'" She rapped the serving spoon on the edge of the lasagna pan and waved it about for emphasis. "That Solo dug up all my flower beds. I worked so hard to plant those petunias and make that garden look nice. It's not fair that the dog ruined it all in one afternoon."

"Mom, your lasagna is the *best*," said Matt, opening his mouth to wolf down a forkful.

"Absolutely," David agreed. "Nobody makes lasagna like your lasagna!"

Megan's mouth was already full, but she lifted her plate slightly to display the tasty mound of lasagna and nodded in the throes of rapture, making loud "mmm-mmm" noises.

"Don't change the subject," said Lainee.

Megan, Matt, and David looked down at their plates, quite sheepishly. None of them were about to defend Solo's rampage through the petunias.

"I am so very sorry about your petunias," said David. "And I'm sure that Solo is sorry too. But what should we do about it?"

"The dog needs training," said Lainee. "And since nobody here seems willing to take responsibility, I'm hiring a dog trainer."

"Mom!" Megan balked. "We only got the dog yesterday! You haven't even given us a chance to make him behave!"

"I see a problem; I take action," said Lainee. "I'm like the Marines."

"But do we really need to hire a dog trainer, honey?" asked David. "Give the dog a chance. He's only been here a day."

Lainee set the serving spoon aside. "Have you seen your favorite running shoes lately?" she asked David, smiling sweetly.

David looked grim. "What happened to my running shoes?"

Lainee stepped away from the table and reached inside the kitchen door. "I found one by the washing machine," she said, returning in a moment with a half-eaten sneaker. "We may never know what happened to the other shoe." She dangled the sad, mangled shoe by a shoelace. Megan and Matt reacted with a pronounced "Euw!"

David pouted disapprovingly. "Okay, you're right," he said with resignation. "Do you want me to look into dog trainers?"

"I pulled three names off the Internet this afternoon," said Lainee. "They're coming by for interviews this weekend."

"This weekend!" Megan protested. "But Mom—!"

"Okay by me!" Matt interjected. "I don't have time to train a dog."

"Not like you would anyway!" argued Megan.

"Enough," said David, silencing his kids with a quick sweep of his fork. "End of discussion."

"But there never *was* a discussion," said Megan.

"Enough!" David repeated—and Megan fell silent.

"Gee, I make great lasagna," said Lainee, adjusting her napkin and raising her fork over the plate.

That weekend, Matt was shooting hoops in the driveway when he noticed a car pull alongside the curb. A pleasant-looking young woman stepped out of the vehicle and approached the Merrill house. She paused along the walkway and called to Matt across the lawn. "Excuse me," she said.

Matt stopped bouncing the basketball and looked in her direction.

"Yeah?" he said.

"Is this four fifty-two Morton Street?" the woman asked.

"Yeah," said Matt.

"Thank you," said the woman, in a

somewhat official tone, and she continued toward the front door.

Matt watched as his mother opened the door, greeted the young woman, and escorted her inside. Then he slipped around to the back door and ran up the back stairs. He hurried down the hall to Megan's room. When he didn't find her inside her room, he headed for the upstairs bathroom. Megan had been hogging the bathroom more than usual lately.

Matt pounded hard enough to make the bathrobes fall off their hooks on the other side of the door. He had discovered that was the only way he could get Megan's attention when she locked herself in the bathroom.

The door opened with a jerk. "What?" said Megan, clearly peeved by the interruption.

"Why don't you just put your pillow in the bathtub and move all your stuff into the bathroom?" said Matt.

"Because I don't *want* to," said Megan. "Is that all you interrupted me for?"

"Mom's interviewing a dog trainer downstairs," said Matt.

Megan gasped with alarm. "Why didn't you tell me?" she cried, pushing past Matt and hurrying down the hall.

"I think I just did!" Matt shouted, following close on his sister's heels all the way downstairs.

"Here they are," said Lainee, as her children appeared in the living room archway. "My daughter, Megan, and my son, Matt."

"Hello," said the young woman sitting on the sofa. She stood up and held out her hand.

"Megan, Matt," said Lainee, "this is Hillary. She's a dog trainer!"

"Actually," Hillary said, raising a finger for a point of correction, "I'm really more of a dog *consultant*."

"'A dog consultant,'" Lainee repeated with enthusiasm. "Oh, really!?" She gestured for her children to sit down and join them. "Hillary and I have been having the most interesting conversation."

"I am not convinced that anyone can ever really *train* an animal to do *any*thing," Hillary continued. "After all, animals are creatures with their own free wills. Just like you and me. We do what we want."

Megan and Matt exchanged a quizzical look. "I can't do what I want," said Megan.

"If I do what I want," said Matt, "I get in trouble."

"Oh, a dog does too," said Hillary. "But the difference is—we know right from wrong, don't we? I don't think dogs always understand what we want them to do. I think they get confused."

Megan looked at her mother and then looked back at Hillary. Then she looked back at her mother again. "What the heck is she talking about?" Megan said in sign language. "I thought dog trainers taught dogs to sit and be quiet and roll over and do tricks."

"Me too," signed Matt.

Lainee gestured for her children to be quiet and kept her focus on Hillary. "Matt and Megan—and I," she explained, "we want to know if you're going to teach Solo how to sit and behave and—well—do tricks."

Hillary winced ever so slightly. "I don't really believe in *tricks*," she said. "What I try to do is to *improve communication*."

"'Improve communication'?" Lainee repeated Hillary's words as a question.

"Yes, quite right," said Hillary. "If you think about it, any discipline problem with a dog can be traced to a failure of communication. In the first place, we don't speak the same language as dogs so they can't understand what we're saying. In the second place, I believe many dogs have been given the wrong name! So the dog you're talking to might not realize you're talking to *him*—because you're not using its correct name."

Megan turned toward her mother and screwed up her lips. "Is she saying we gave Solo the wrong name?" Megan asked in sign language. "'Solo' is a *great* name. It's the *perfect* name!"

"I mean, for all we know, your dog thinks you're talking to some *other* dog," Hillary continued. "So the very first thing I do is to determine if your dog has been given its rightful name."

"And how do you do that?" asked Lainee.

"I gaze into the dog's eyes until the dog tells me its *true* name," Hillary said quite simply, "whatever that might be."

"'Whatever that might be,'" Lainee repeated.

"Actually, I'm more of an animal *psychic*, really," Hillary said with a shy smile.

"An 'animal psychic'?" Matt repeated, definitely puzzled.

"Yes," said Hillary. "Animals tell me what they're thinking, and then I help them to understand what we want them to do. Most animals are grateful for the clarification."

Megan nudged Matt and dropped her fist on his knee, over and over again. Matt glanced down to see that Megan was tapping out the letters to a word in the manual alphabet.

K O O K

"I don't mind a dog trainer necessarily," said Megan, "but I don't want Solo trained by an animal *kook*!"

"I'm not sure I like that word," said Lainee.

"Mom," Megan protested, "she was a *nut*!"

"She *was* pretty nutty," said Matt, "but I say, let her train the dog."

"Matt!" Megan balked. "You're not serious!"

"Hey, I've got softball practice after school and every weekend afternoon for the next couple months!" Matt argued. "I don't have time to train the dog—much less walk him, feed him, and give him his bath. And *you* won't do it, I know!"

"What do you mean I 'won't do it'?" Megan protested. "You haven't even given me a chance!"

Lainee waved her arms to end the brother-sister bickering. "Look," she cried, "we're seeing two more dog trainers today! I'll admit Hillary wasn't what we were looking for—but maybe one of the other two will work out!"

"Maybe," Megan allowed—but she briefly crossed her fingers behind her back, hoping that they wouldn't. She didn't like the idea of someone else telling her how to raise Solo. She dropped to one knee and looked deeply into Solo's eyes. "What do *you* think of the idea?" she asked Solo. The dog didn't say anything in response but Megan could tell that he didn't like the idea. *I want* you *to train me.* That's what Megan imagined Solo meant to say as the dog craned his neck forward to lick her face.

Megan threw her arm around the dog's neck and tugged him closer beside her in the front hall. "Don't you worry," she said. "The only person who gets to read your mind—is *me.*"

In response, Solo barked loudly—but Megan soon realized that the dog was barking because someone was at the front door. Matt ran to answer the door—and Megan knew to get their mother. She charged down the hall with the dog leaping about her heels.

"Mom," she cried, flinging herself into the doorway to the kitchen. "Dog trainer at the door." She and Solo disappeared down the hall to get a look at the new arrival before Lainee could respond.

When Lainee arrived in the living room, Megan and Matt were sitting on either side of a young man wearing a big broad smile. Solo sat on the carpet at their feet, and the young man scratched the dog under its chin.

"Mom, this is Bailey," said Matt.

"Howdy, ma'am," said the young man, rising from the sofa and extending his hand. "Bailey Simms."

"A pleasure to meet you, Bailey," said Lainee. "As I'm sure my children have explained, we hope to hire a dog trainer."

"And I am the man for the job," said Bailey. "This is one beautiful dog." He scratched Solo behind the ears. Solo growled contentedly and issued two happy yips.

"Thank you," said Lainee. "And you are a dog *trainer*?" She emphasized the specific occupation to make sure she wasn't getting another "consultant" or a "psychic."

"A dog trainer, ma'am, and so much more," Bailey said with enthusiasm. "I'll teach Solo how to behave. How to walk, how to heel, and how to stay. And I'll teach him a few tricks besides. Roll over, shake hands, jump on command. The usual stuff."

"Oh, good," Lainee responded, smiling at Megan and Matt. "Better and better!"

"And you don't have to walk him if you don't want to," said Bailey. "I'll come by and take care of that. And I might as well feed him while I'm here."

"Great!" said Matt.

"Yes, well, we were hoping to teach the children responsibility, of course," said Lainee. "So we've already agreed that Megan and Matt will share the chores to make sure that Solo is fed and walked and groomed."

"I could handle the grooming," Bailey offered. "I'm pretty good with a brush and some clippers. And if I'm going to do all that, I might as well give him a bath at the same time."

For a moment, Megan thought it might not be so bad to hire Bailey. He seemed so eager to take care of all the baths and grooming stuff.

"No, just the training, I think," said Lainee. "If Solo is going to be the family dog, I want the kids to take responsibility for raising him."

"Oh, I hear you," said Bailey, nodding in agreement. "But are they going to keep him active? I have a theory that dogs like Solo only misbehave when they're *bored*. If they're not active enough, they're more likely to get into trouble."

"He's only been here a couple days," Lainee responded, "so he hasn't really had a chance to get bored yet."

"Well, if he starts acting up," said Bailey, "my guess is that he's bored. So you let me know if you want me to come over to put in some extra time—oh, you know, playing games, taking walks, reading books, whatever."

"Reading books?" asked Megan. "You read books to a *dog*?"

"Oh, I read to my dogs all the time," said Bailey. "Don't you?"

Matt and Megan exchanged a curious look. They glanced at their mom for guidance but apparently Lainee had already made up her mind.

"Well, thank you so much," said Lainee, rising to her feet. "This has been very informative!" The kids stood beside her.

"Oh, yes! I think this is going to work out just fine!" Bailey enthused, acting as though he'd already been hired. He rose from the sofa and briskly brushed his hands off against his thighs. "The only other thing," he added, "is that once a month, I invite all my dog clients over to my house for a slumber party."

"A slumber party?" asked Lainee, using the same bewildered tone she had with Hillary, the first dog trainer.

"Yes, only a *dog* slumber party," said Bailey. "Just for dogs. No owners allowed! I invite about fifteen dogs, and we play games and watch some television. I serve doggie snacks—and then it's time for beddy-bye."

"Fifteen dogs?" Megan asked her mom in sign language. "He must really like dogs!"

Lainee didn't say anything in response to the slumber parties. She simply opened the front door and said, "Well, my! This has been so interesting!"

"I brought some letters of recommendation," Bailey added, reaching into his satchel to produce a sheath of papers.

"They were written by dog owners—but signed by the dogs." He pointed to smudgy paw prints on the letters.

"What was the matter with *that* guy?" Megan asked after Bailey had pulled away.

"I don't know," said Lainee. "There was just something a little too 'too.'"

"Too 'too' what?" asked Megan.

"Too friendly," Lainee responded.

"That guy needs to get a life!" cried Matt. "It's like his only friends are dogs!"

"'A dog slumber party!'" said Megan, imitating Bailey. She caught herself in the reflection of the oven door and did a dead-on impersonation of the dog trainer. "Does your dog want to come? *You're* not invited! But your *dog* can come! We're going to watch television! And eat snacks! But you can't come!"

"Well, it doesn't matter," said Lainee. "I'd already decided not to hire him. It's perfectly okay if he likes dogs as friends—but Solo happens to be *our* best friend. And we don't have to share him with anybody!"

When Lainee turned her back, Megan poked Matt in the ribs.

"*Ow!* What?" said Matt.

"Mom says, Solo is '*our* best friend,'" Megan said in sign language, grinning broadly.

"Yeah," Matt signed back, "but she also said she and dad are teaching us responsibility."

"So what?" said Megan.

"So we're going to have to share the chores," Matt continued. "That means we walk him and feed him and groom him and bathe him."

"We already said we'd do that," said Megan.

"Yeah, only *you're* not going to do it!" said Matt.

"Yes, I will," said Megan.

"No, you won't," said Matt. "I always end up doing your chores and picking up your mess."

"That's not true," Megan protested.

"It's pretty close to the truth," Matt insisted. "So if we take on a dog, I know what's going to happen. I'm going to be the one who ends up doing all the work!"

"What are you two signing about behind my back?" asked Lainee from the sink.

"Megan's not going to do any of the work raising Solo," said Matt. "It's all going to fall on me!" Matt spoke first—so Megan stuck out her tongue.

"You know I don't like that tongue thing," Lainee said to her daughter. "Megan, Matt says you're not going to help with Solo. Is that true?"

"No!" Megan declared. "I already promised to help bathe him and feed him and train him. What's the point of hiring a trainer? I can take care of Solo all by myself!"

"You want to spend the day teaching the dog how to sit?" Matt argued. "Fine! Knock yourself out. But not me. I've got better things to do."

"There's no point in discussing this now!" said Lainee. "We still have one more dog trainer to interview—and maybe he'll work out fine. Maybe he'll be just right for the job!" At that point, Megan's mom headed down the hall to answer the front door. Matt signed that the doorbell had rung, and Megan nodded.

"We have to do something, Matt," said Megan. "If we don't, Mom might hire one of the awful trainers."

"She already said no to the bad ones," said Matt.

"But if she doesn't hire a trainer,"

Megan insisted, "she might tell Dad we have to get rid of Solo. The dog just got here and—he'll be all alone again!"

Matt didn't answer. Instead he tugged on Megan's sleeve until she was headed down the hall to meet the third dog trainer. They stumbled into the den to find Lainee with a stocky man in a crew cut, waiting somewhat impatiently with his arms crossed. His acrylic name tag read: "Sergeant Darnell."

"Sit! Sit!" Sergeant Darnell commanded, pointing firmly toward the ground.

Lainee, Matt, and Megan promptly sat down on the sofa.

"I didn't mean you," said the man with a gentle laugh. "I meant the *dog*." Lainee, Matt, and Megan shared a little chuckle— but none of them budged.

Solo remained in the archway, halfway to the hall. He glanced warily toward Lainee, Matt, and Megan, seated on the sofa. Solo didn't budge either.

"I like to think of myself as the doggie drill sergeant," Darnell began, reaching for Solo's collar to drag him into the room.

Once Solo was positioned in front of the

sofa, Sergeant Darnell pressed down firmly on Solo's tail end, saying, "Sit, sit"—until the dog was seated on the carpet. When Solo held the position, Darnell barked, "Good dog! Good dog!" but he didn't sound especially nice about it.

As soon as Darnell released his hand, Solo's rump rose again until the dog was standing on all fours. Matt started to snicker and shake at the sight—which only made Megan giggle too. Lainee had to lift a single finger to her lips to indicate, "Shhhhh."

"I believe in zero tolerance; don't you worry," Darnell declared, squatting low on the floor and pressing Solo's rump once more until the dog was seated. "A couple weeks with me and this dog won't give you any more guff at all."

Sure enough, as soon as Darnell stood on his feet and turned his back, Solo rose on all fours again. Matt and Megan started to laugh. When Darnell noticed that the dog was standing, he pointed to the floor and began to bark. "Sit, Solo, sit! Sit, Solo, sit!"

"Yes, well, thank you very much," said Lainee, interrupting the demonstration. "We really do appreciate the trouble you took to visit us today. We'll make our decision and give you a call." She rose from the sofa to lead Darnell to the door.

As soon as Darnell and Lainee had left the room, Solo trotted around the coffee table and began to lick Megan's hands.

"Sergeant Darnell reminds me of you," said Matt.

"What's that supposed to mean?" asked Megan.

"He's bossy like you," Matt replied.

"I'm not bossy with Solo," Megan protested.

"You're bossy with everybody else," said Matt.

Megan balled up a fist and pretended to sock Matt in the shoulder but she shook her hand free when her mother returned to the room.

"Mom!" cried Megan. "Matt says I'm as bossy as Sergeant Darnell."

Lainee ignored the comment altogether. She was focused on the matter at hand. "So-o-o-o," she began, drawing out the syllable for as long as it took to cross the room and flop back down on the sofa. "What did you two think of the dog trainers?"

"One was too nutty," said Megan.

"Hillary. The psychic one."

"And one was too friendly," added Matt. "Bailey. A dog's best friend."

"And one was too strict," Lainee concluded. "Sergeant Darnell. So what do we do? Which one do we hire?"

"Not the nutty one!" said Megan.

"Not the friendly one!" said Matt. "I guess it's okay if you want to hire the strict guy. He'll get the job done."

Megan shrugged in a way that meant she agreed.

"Yes, but I'm not sure *I* could take it," said Lainee. "Your father and I have always been firm but not 'strict' with you children. I can't imagine your father wants me to hire someone that strict for our dog," said Lainee.

"So you're not going to hire any of the dog trainers?" asked Megan.

"We're going to keep looking," said Lainee. "In the meantime, I expect both of you—Megan and Matt—to stay on top of Solo. He needs to be bathed; he needs to be fed; he needs to be walked—and I don't want him digging up my petunias!"

"We will," said Megan.

"You mean *I* will," Matt said to Megan. "You say you will but you'll lose interest after a week!"

"No, I won't," Megan argued.

"No empty promises," said Lainee in a tone that was firm without being strict. "I need a commitment!"

"Okay!" said Megan. "I swear! I double-swear! I double-triple-swear!"

"No empty promises and no jokes, either," said Lainee. "We're going to approach this situation on a trial basis. You two have to prove that you're up to the challenge."

"What challenge?" asked Megan.

"She's talking about Solo," said Matt. "Taking care of the dog."

"Oh, yeah," said Megan. "I knew that." She wrapped an arm around Solo's neck and drew him close. "I love you, Solo!" she cooed into the dog's ear.

"It's not a matter of how much we love the dog," said Lainee. "It's whether we can give him a good home. And that means you and your brother have to be responsible."

"Yes, ma'am," said Megan.

"Nice try on the 'I love you, Solo!' routine," said Matt. Megan kept her attention on her mother and pretended not to understand her brother's remark.

"I don't want any fighting over whose turn it is to take care of the dog. I just want a happy, clean, well-fed, well-behaved dog," said Lainee. "Do you understand?"

Megan and Matt nodded.

"In a couple weeks, your father and I will review the situation," Lainee continued. "And then we'll decide."

"Decide what?" asked Megan.

"Whether or not we keep the dog," Lainee stated with emphasis.

Megan clutched Solo even tighter. She widened her eyes, batted her lashes, and twisted her lips into an adorable pout as though she and the dog were being photographed for a dog food commercial.

"I'm not falling for the 'puppy dog' face," said Lainee, rising from the sofa and crossing toward the hall. "Just do the job."

Megan and Matt watched their mother climb the stairs until they were alone in the living room with the dog.

Megan pointed a finger at Matt and used the same finger to poke herself in the chest. "So it's up to us," she signed. "It's up to you and me."

Matt shook his head from side to side.

"Wrong," he said. "I'll do my share but it's like I told you before. I have softball practice and games and things to do. So don't expect me to do it all."

Megan was ready to argue the point, but Matt got off the sofa and left the room with a sense of purpose, as if he was demonstrating how seriously busy he suddenly was. Megan was left alone on the sofa with Solo— and her finger still pointing at her chest.

"Okay, Solo," she said simply. "I guess it's up to me."

EIGHT
STAY

The next day, Megan and Solo were having a stare down.

"Made you blink," said Megan, when Solo flinched and looked away. She kept her gaze locked on to Solo's big brown eyes. Sure enough, Solo fidgeted and turned away.

"Made you blink again," said Megan.

Solo reached out his paw and impatiently tapped Megan's arm. He lifted his head and yipped twice. It was dog-speak for "I'm tired of this! Let's do something else!"

Megan continued to stare. She had won the title at summer camp for "Stare Down Champion of the Western Hemisphere." Megan was a determined competitor when it came to a stare down. She played to win.

But Solo didn't want to play at all. He licked his chops in a way that suggested an interest in anything but the competition. He nudged Megan's chin with his cold wet nose, urging her to end the game.

"No, you're not supposed to touch me," Megan insisted. "That's cheating. Now, look at me. Look at me."

Solo quit. The dog was so frustrated with the game that he refused to look at Megan at all. Solo looked at the wall and the window and the clock.

"No, Solo," said Megan. "*Me*. Look at me." She grabbed his chin and gestured from the dog's eyes to her own. It was the same sign language that people use for "look at me."

And it seemed to work. Solo returned the stare down for ten full seconds before he finally caved, and Megan won her sixth consecutive stare down championship title.

Matt walked into the room with a sandwich. "Stop torturing the dog," he said, as he flopped into a chair.

"I'm not torturing him," said Megan. "I taught him a trick."

"You can't teach that dog anything,"

Matt groused. "I tried for two hours yester-day to teach him how to 'stay.' 'Stay!' How hard is that? But Solo would not do it."

"Did you teach him with words?" said Megan.

"Yes, what else?" said Matt between bites.

"He doesn't speak words," Megan replied. "You have to teach him in sign."

"Solo knows sign language? We've only been training him ourselves for a day and a half, and you already taught him sign lan-guage?"

"I taught him 'look at me,'" said Megan. "Watch." She repeated the gestures for "look at me"—and, sure enough, Solo did.

"That's a fluke," said Matt.

"You try it," said Megan.

Matt wolfed down the rest of his sand-wich in one bite and—with his cheeks still bulging—he signed "look at me" to the dog.

Solo looked.

"Huh," said Matt, mumbling over a big mouthful of food. "Maybe we've been doing it wrong. We've been teaching Solo with words when we should have been using sign."

"I did not understand a single word you

just said," Megan replied. "And neither did Solo."

Matt swallowed and tried again. "Maybe I could get him to do a few tricks with sign language," he said.

"Oh sure," said Megan. "Now that you know about sign language, the whole dog-training thing just got more interesting, right?"

Megan holed up with Solo in her bedroom for more than an hour that afternoon, determined to see if sign language would get him to obey. "I want you to know I'm the boss," she said both out loud and in sign.

Solo danced back a few steps and then *sat*—staring back at Megan as intently as before. It might have been dog-speak for "yeah, yeah, okay"—but Megan couldn't be sure.

This time, instead of speaking out loud, Megan simply signed, "I want you to know I'm the boss."

Solo watched her movements and stayed in his place, still staring intently. He didn't get up and walk away as Megan would have done if anyone had ever insisted that he or she was the boss over her. Solo stayed—

seeming to understand that Megan was, in fact, the boss. His willingness to participate also suggested, to Megan anyway, that he understood everything she had said. Everything she had *signed*.

"Okay, then," Megan continued, rising to her feet, "I'm going to teach you to sit on command."

When Megan stood, the dog followed. He was eager to play but Megan remained tough. "Sit, Solo, sit!" she commanded.

Sign language for "sit" was to place two extended fingers of her right hand across two extended fingers of her left hand, with both palms facing down. Megan repeated the gesture and pushed firmly on Solo's rump until he was sitting.

Megan repeated the lesson over and over again until Solo started hunkering down the moment he saw the sign rather than waiting for Megan to push on his rump. And whenever that happened, Megan praised him with a vigorous rub and a kiss on the head.

Of course, all the affection invariably got Solo back onto his feet again and the "sit, Solo, sit!" lesson started all over again.

After a while, Megan decided to advance

to "stay." She firmly held out the palm of her hand as though she was freezing Solo into position. It took Solo a while to make sense of the sign for "stay"—but actually, less time in the long run than it took to learn "sit."

Once Megan felt that Solo was comfortable with the commands for "sit" and "stay," she tried "lie down," which meant getting Solo to spread out on the floor. The sign for "lie down" was to rest her cheek against her right palm, almost as if she was going to sleep.

Solo wasn't very interested in learning to lie down. Try as she might, Megan couldn't get it to happen. Solo was happy enough to sit and stay—and he clearly wasn't ready to lie down anytime soon.

"Okay, okay," said Megan. "I guess 'sit' and 'stay' are enough for your first lesson. Do it again. Sit, Solo, sit! Stay!"

Solo did.

The funny thing was—now that Megan could get Solo to "sit" and "stay," she didn't know what else to do with him. She turned her back and walked across the room, and when she turned around again, Solo was still sitting there, still waiting patiently for Megan to ask him to do something.

Maybe he thinks he's an audience, thought

Megan. *He's waiting for the show!*

The idea was so excellent that Megan had to applaud. Unfortunately, her applause brought Solo back onto his feet, and Megan had to settle him down all over again by repeating the sign language for "sit, Solo, sit!" and "stay!"

Once Solo held his position again, Megan strode across the room to an open area beside her bed. She turned to face Solo and began.

"Good afternoon, my name is Megan Merrill," she said. "My audition for the role of Dorothy in the class production of *Wizard!*, based on *The Wizard of Oz*, will be two songs. First, I will perform 'Let There Be Peace on Earth.' And for my second song, I will perform 'She'll Be Coming Round the Mountain.'"

Solo hadn't flinched or fidgeted. It seemed as if he couldn't wait for the show to begin.

So Megan began. "Let there be peace on earth," she sang soulfully with her hands, "and let it begin with me." She threw her whole heart into it.

When she reached the end, she was afraid to applaud for herself—for fear of Solo's jumping and barking again. Instead

Megan took a moment, composed herself, and launched into the rowdier song "She'll Be Coming Round the Mountain."

Solo could tell from Megan's movements that the mood had changed. The dog got rambunctious too, prancing on the carpet with his front paws and yipping enthusiastically when Megan pointed at him to bark in time to the music.

After the run-through, Megan gave Solo a big hug. She was feeling a lot more confident about her performance even though it felt strange not to see her reflection in the mirror while she was singing.

Megan felt certain that Ms. Scherer would recognize that she had what it took to play Dorothy. *Even so,* Megan thought, *it would be nice to perform for someone other than a dog.*

She had to practice on people.

"Mom!" Megan hollered, running from the room and charging downstairs.

"Mom!" Megan continued to yell over the roar of the vacuum. Lainee didn't hear her daughter at first because she was concentrating on the dust bunnies under the television set in the den.

To get her attention, Megan unplugged the vacuum cleaner.

"Whaaa—?" Lainee asked, as she stood

and twisted toward the wall with the electrical outlet.

"Mom, I need your help," said Megan.

"Can it wait till I finish vacuuming?"

"No, Mom," said Megan, "it can't wait." She took her mother by the elbow and forced her to sit down on the sofa. "I'm auditioning for the class play, and I need you to watch my audition."

"Yes, yes, yes," said Lainee, still distracted by the vacuum cord. "*The Wizard of Oz*. Which part are you going to play?"

"They haven't decided yet, Mom!" Megan said with impatience. "That's why we have to 'audition'!"

"Yes but—which part do you *want* to play?" asked Lainee.

"Mom," Megan asserted, as though the answer was obvious. "If I don't get to play Dorothy, I'm going to lock myself in my room and hold my breath until I turn purple! So you'd better hope I get Dorothy!"

"Dorothy!?!" said Lainee with surprise and delight.

"The play hasn't even been cast, Mom," said Megan. "Let me get through my audition."

"Where do you want me to sit?" said Lainee, even as she plopped down on the sofa and folded her hands on her lap, fully prepared to be a well-behaved and attentive audience member.

"Okay," said Megan, standing in front of the television set as if she was appearing onstage. "Hello, my name is Megan Merrill. For my first song, I'd like to sing—"

Her audition was interrupted by a knock at the door.

"Hang on, honey," said Lainee. "Somebody's at the door." Her mother rose from the sofa and walked to the front hall.

"Ugh!" Megan grunted, following her mother. "Who could that be?"

Nothing could have prepared Megan for the surprise that was waiting. When her mother opened the front door, there stood *Lizzie*.

"Surprise!" said Lizzie.

Surprise in sign language is expressed by flicking two fingers above both eyes—indicating the way eyes get really big with surprise—which is exactly what happened to Megan when she saw Lizzie at the front door.

Both girls screamed. They flung their arms around each other's necks, jumping up and down and roaring with laughter.

Lizzie's mother stepped into view at the front door, smiling sweetly. She extended her hand toward Lainee. "I'm Brenda Rappaport, Lizzie's mother."

"Yes, I certainly recognize Lizzie from the computer screen," said Lainee. "And I think we've almost said hello a few times in the background when the girls have been speaking on that video-relay thing."

"Yes, but please don't ask me to explain how that works," Brenda said, laughing.

"Oh, I know!" said Lainee. "Me neither!"

"But what are you doing here?" Megan signed to Lizzie.

"We moved!" replied Lizzie.

"You moved?" Lainee asked Brenda.

"Yes, we moved," said Brenda.

"Not only that," Lizzie continued, "but I'm starting at your school."

"*You're* going to *my* school?" Megan cried. The girls started laughing, screaming, and hugging all over again.

"My husband got transferred to a new office on this side of the city," Brenda explained, "and, rather than commute, we agreed to move Lizzie into Megan's school district so that she could be in the same school as her friend."

"Well, it's a very good school," said Lainee. "You're going to be very happy. Wilmot Elementary has a wonderful program for students who are hearing deaf."

"Oh, I did my research on Wilmot Elementary," said Brenda. "Believe you me."

"My school is so cool," said Megan. "And you've come at the best possible time! You're not going to believe what's happening. Our classroom is putting on a stage production of *The Wizard of Oz*!"

"No way!" cried Lizzie. "I love *The Wizard of Oz*!"

"We call it *Wizard!* and I'm auditioning for Dorothy!" Megan blurted in her excitement.

"Oh, I want to audition for Dorothy too!" said Lizzie.

Megan smiled—but it was a frozen smile. She was so surprised by Lizzie's response that she couldn't think of a thing to say.

She was disappointed, of course, that Lizzie would want to audition for Dorothy. She didn't like the idea that she and Lizzie would be in competition for the same part. And she also didn't like the idea that anyone would compete with her for the part of Dorothy at all. At the same time, she couldn't have been happier to see Lizzie. It was all so confusing.

To make matters worse, Lizzie's mother jumped onto the bandwagon. "Oh, Lizzie," she said, "you would make a wonderful Dorothy!"

"Well, I suppose they each would make a wonderful Dorothy!" said Lainee, crossing her fingers for good luck. "We'll just have to keep our fingers crossed for the audition!"

"Fingers and toes," said Megan.

"So when are the auditions?" asked Lizzie.

Megan flinched. Lizzie already knew what an "audition" was. Lizzie probably had an audition all prepared!

"Oh, sometime next week," said Megan.

"I thought you said auditions were on Wednesday," said Lainee.

"Oh, yeah," said Megan. "It's Wednesday. They're on Wednesday."

"So soon!" said Brenda, wrapping her arm around Lizzie. "Lizzie, we'll have to spend some time preparing a good audition for you over the next couple of days!"

Lizzie nodded eagerly. Megan realized

she was still wearing her frozen smile.

A split second later, Brenda let out a little moan of disappointment. "Oh, no—actually, Wednesday might be a little crazy," Brenda said. "We're dealing with the moving trucks on Wednesday, Wednesday is supposed to be Lizzie's official first day back in school, and the cable is being connected on Wednesday afternoon!" Lizzie's mother had a way of sounding all business and all party, both at the same time.

"Wednesday should be an exciting day!" said Lainee.

"Yes, but maybe already too exciting to include an audition," said Brenda.

Lizzie looked disappointed. "But, Mom—!" she protested.

"Don't worry about it," said Megan. "It's no big deal. Just wait till you see our school! I've got my own interpreter and everything. And you're going to go crazy for my friends. You're going to love it all."

Lizzie smiled gamely—and Megan smiled back.

NINE
THANK YOU, NEXT!

Have you noticed," said Cindy, clutching her copy of *The Wizard of Oz*, "that the Wicked Witch of the West isn't nearly so wicked in the book? She's really not as bad as you'd think."

That Wednesday morning, Megan and Cindy stood by the Wilmot Elementary flagpole waiting for the bell but Megan wasn't really paying attention to her friend. She was concentrating on the small stretch of road in front of their school. She brightened considerably when a bright red sedan pulled up to the curb.

"The Good Witch is named Glinda in the movie but not in the book," Cindy continued, "and in the book, it's the Tin

Woodman, not the Tin Man. And the Flying Monkeys are Winged Monkeys, but they still fly all the same."

"Whatever," said Megan.

"You're not listening to me," said Cindy. "You have to look at me to listen to me."

"Hey, Cindy," said Megan. "Recognize the new girl?"

"Where?" asked Cindy.

Megan put her hands on Cindy's shoulders and spun her around so that she was facing the street. Two large school buses remained at the curb. Safety guards in Day-Glo vests supervised the flow of moms and dads in the morning run, waiting in a long line of cars to drop off their kids.

Megan had hardly been able to contain herself the night before when she had instant-messaged Cindy on the computer about homework assignments. She hadn't told her friend about her great idea to use the camp songs for her audition, and she hadn't mentioned a word about Lizzie.

But when Lizzie stepped out of her dad's car in front of the school, Megan had to spill the beans of the big surprise.

"Which girl where?" said Cindy.

"That girl there," Megan said, pointing

directly at Lizzie. "The one who looks like—
Lizzie." As they watched, the girl who had
just stepped out of the red sedan tapped the
car door to let her dad know she was safely
on the sidewalk and turned to face the
school.

"Omigosh, it's Lizzie!" Cindy screamed.

"Lizzie!" cried Megan, just for the sheer
joy of it.

The two girls ran toward their friend
and formed a tight circle, shrieking with
happiness and exchanging hugs. "What are
you doing here?" Cindy signed to Lizzie.

"I live here!" signed Lizzie.

"Lizzie's dad got transferred, but never
mind about that," said Megan. "She's here
now, so what does it matter?"

"Lizzie, *here*?" Cindy cried. "In our
school?!"

"She's standing right in front of you,"
said Megan. "Yes, she's here!"

"You girls better brace yourselves!" said
Lizzie. "You just got a new best friend!"

The girls started screaming again. By
the time the first bell rang, all the kids had
poured off the playground and pushed past
the school doors. Megan, Cindy, and Lizzie
were the last to enter.

"So you guys are going to look out for me, right?" said Lizzie, as they headed for the classroom. "I'm a little freaked out by the 'new' house, 'new' school, 'new' teacher, 'new' friends."

"Don't you worry," said Megan. "Your new friends are our old friends—and they're going to like you as much as we do!"

Ms. Endee invited Lizzie to stand at the front of the classroom for her official introduction—and then assigned her a seat near the door. "I know you and Megan are friends," said Ms. Endee, "but we're here to get an education—so I'm seating you two at opposite ends of the room because I don't trust you girls together!" It was sort of funny, but Megan could tell that Ms. Endee meant it too. Even though they were across the room from each other, both girls remained in full view of Jann for the sign language translations.

The next hour was spent reviewing prefixes, suffixes, synonyms, and antonyms. At the end of the period, Ms. Endee closed her English textbook and directed the students to line up at the classroom door.

"Where are we going?" asked Ronnie

Jiu. "What are we doing? What's going on?"

"Our auditions for *Wizard! The Wizard of Oz!* Don't you remember?" Ms. Endee announced.

Again, right on cue, Ms. Scherer stepped into the door frame. She was wearing another brightly colored floral dress—but today her hair was pulled back as though she meant business. She clutched a clipboard to her chest, one pencil was tucked behind her ear, and two more pencils were entwined between her fingers.

The students roared with excitement—although some moaned fretfully at the prospect of performing in front of their friends. Jann counted the number of heads in the room and signaled the sum to Ms. Scherer.

"I reserved the auditorium so we could hold auditions on the same stage where we'd be performing," Ms. Endee continued. "Once we get to the auditorium, Ms. Scherer is in charge, and what she says goes. So bring whatever you might need for your audition because we are leaving the classroom and not coming back until after the auditions!"

The students chattered nervously as

they gathered whatever props they needed.

"People! People!" Ms. Scherer called. "Now, I count twenty-seven—no, twenty-*eight*—students in this class and, if you do the math, we only have so much time to hold these auditions. So I need you to listen respectfully, and I need you to behave. I know nobody wants to go first, so when we get to the auditorium, I'm going to call names at random. Everyone has to pay attention and be prepared—because your name could be called next!"

Ms. Endee had a few more comments about behavior but it all went in one ear and out the other as the students headed for the auditorium.

Once they reached the space, Ms. Scherer asked the students to sit in the first three rows.

Cindy and Megan found Lizzie and tugged her along to sit with Alexis and Bethany so that the Leading Ladies could stick together in the second row. As it happened, Cindy was positioned directly behind Ms. Scherer's seat with a full view of the notepad on Ms. Scherer's clipboard. Cindy elbowed Megan and slyly pointed one finger in the direction of Ms. Scherer's pad.

Megan offered a thumbs-up—but also moved one finger to her lips for "Shhhhh."

Jann took her position at the far end of the stage so that she could translate the auditions into sign language. "First up, Frankie Adams," said Ms. Scherer, referring to her list. "And Alexis, you're next!"

Alexis jumped from her seat and crawled over the girls sitting beside her, tapping crossed fingers for good luck as she passed.

Frankie Adams slipped out of the row in front of them and marched down the aisle to mount the stairs that led to the stage. He kept one arm cocked behind his back as if he was hiding something. When he reached the center of the stage, he turned to face the audience and said, "Hello, my name is Frankie Adams."

"What have you got for us, Frankie?" said Ms. Scherer.

Frankie surprised everyone by pulling out a baton and *twirling* it. The surprise wasn't just the baton—but how good he was at it. Clearly, Frankie had been practicing a lot. Even better than the twirling was the fact that Frankie managed to twirl and *talk* at the same time. He tossed the baton into the air—and before he caught it, he began to recite *The Declaration of Independence*.

Megan and Cindy had to admit it was impressive to watch Frankie as he flung the baton around his neck and between his legs and even threw it overhead, without missing a word and without interrupting the twirling. Even so, Cindy leaned against Megan and signed, "It's cool about the baton, but how many times is Frankie going to make us listen to *The Declaration of Independence*?"

"I know," Megan agreed, explaining to Lizzie, "anytime we have to recite something, Frankie always pulls out the good old *Declaration of Independence*. It's the only thing he knows by heart!"

Frankie got a round of applause when he finished, and it seemed as if the auditions were off to a great start.

Alexis surprised everyone by walking onstage playing "When the Saints Go Marching In" on her father's French horn, slightly off-key, but very enthusiastic. It was a practically perfect performance. When her audition was over, the girls cheered for Alexis. Cindy happened to notice Ms. Scherer write on her pad: "Where to put the

French horn? Munchkins? Emerald City? Inside tornado?"

Each audition seemed to hold its own surprise. Lillian Olan walked onstage in a tutu, tiptoeing in toe shoes. Dwight McNamara walked onstage on his hands. Tracy Benz zipped across the stage on roller skates. Keisha Dunbar did a rather remarkable dance with a rhythmic ribbon wand from gymnastics to "This Land Is Your Land" and Enrique Lopez walked on stilts! Each time, the students roared with approval.

Of course, there were a few clunkers. Donny Vargas strutted onstage with his arms and legs as stiff as a robot's. "Abracadabra," said Donny, as he pulled a floral bouquet out of his pocket—and scores of playing cards, red rubber balls, and wildly colorful scarves abruptly tumbled from his pockets, sleeves, and trouser legs. All the kids laughed and applauded anyway—and Cindy noticed Ms. Scherer jot the words "potential Wizard?" on her pad.

Some of the kids chose to audition in teams. Tracy returned to the stage with Sawyer Michner to demonstrate a few karate moves. Tracy threw a few kicks and

Sawyer ducked. Then Sawyer charged Tracy, but he got thrown on his back. When they were through, Cindy spotted Ms. Scherer writing down, "Definitely Flying Monkeys." So far, Cindy had observed that any kid with a somersault, a cartwheel, or a forward roll was automatically drafted for the Flying Monkeys.

The twosome was followed by a threesome. Trina Stehr, Elizabeth Watts, and Bethany York performed a terrific double-Dutch jump-rope routine that most of the class was already familiar with from the playground, but it was still exciting to see it performed onstage. When it was over, Cindy saw Ms. Scherer quickly scribble, "Jump-rope kids? Tornado???"

Tony Rosenblum took his good sweet time walking onstage when his name was called. He introduced himself from center stage—and then he started his favorite joke. "Why did the chicken cross the road?" Tony asked.

"Why?" the audience responded.

"Don't ask me; ask the chicken!" said Tony. Kids laughed and groaned—and Tony dove into another joke. "Why did the cow cross the road?"

"Why?" the audience said again.

"To get to the udder side," said Tony.

Kids laughed at the joke and how *bad* the joke was.

Tony had more. "Why did the sheep cross the road?"

"Why?" the audience responded.

"To go to the baa-baa shop!"

The laughter got louder as the jokes got worse.

"Thank you!" cried Ms. Scherer. "Enough! You're killing me!"

"Just one more," said Tony. "Why did the fish cross the ocean?"

Of course the audience replied, "Why?"

"To get to the other *tide*," said Tony.

As Tony left the stage, Lizzie turned to Megan and said, "His jokes are awful but he's very funny." Cindy snuck a peek at Ms. Scherer's pad and saw that she had written, "possible Wizard?"

Megan and Cindy squirmed in their seats when Casey took the stage. They had already decided that Casey should be cast as the Tin Woodman because she was so tall and she wore braces on her teeth. Megan still cringed at the thought of braces.

Casey stood center stage and announced,

"I don't really have any special talent, but I am *double-jointed*." If kids didn't know what "double-jointed" meant, they were about to find out. Casey proceeded to bend back her wrist so that her finger almost touched her forearm. Then she pulled her thumb forward so that it touched the underside of her forearm. And then she extended both arms and arched them so that they appeared to bend slightly backward.

The kids reacted with loud groans at first—but by the time Casey finished, they watched with quiet fascination. "How does she *do* that?" asked Cindy.

"I don't know," said Megan. "But she's the Tin Woodman for sure."

"You don't think maybe the Scarecrow instead?" said Cindy.

"See what Ms. Scherer wrote on her pad," signed Megan.

Cindy leaned forward to peek but she was distracted by a really loud sneeze. Ronnie Jiu was climbing the steps to the stage but stopped halfway to pull out a large handkerchief and release a big rattling sneeze; the kind that stops a kid in his tracks.

"Gesundheit," said Ms. Scherer.

"Thanks," said Ronnie, tucking away the handkerchief and continuing onto the stage. When he reached the audition spot in the center, Ronnie turned to face the audience—and sneezed again. In fact, he sneezed four more times in quick succession, so hard that it rattled his body down to his sneakers.

"Gesundheit," said the audience. *"Gesundheit, gesundheit, gesundheit."*

Ronnie said, "Thanks . . . thanks, thanks, thanks"—and then he took a little bow as though his audition was over and said, "thank you."

"That's it?" asked Ms. Scherer.

"That's it. That's my special skill," said Ronnie. "I sneeze." Even as Ronnie was saying the word, another sneeze appeared to be rising inside him. Ronnie shook his handkerchief like a pom-pom as his face twitched and contorted this way and that. He found a stool onstage and gripped it tightly for balance. All the kids in the audience cringed, anticipating a full-scale level 5 hurricane of a sneeze—but still giggling despite themselves. When the sneeze arrived, of course, it was barely more than a whimper. "Excuse me," said

Ronnie, wiping away a sniffle.

"Gesundheit," said Ms. Scherer, with an arched eyebrow. "Quite the little comedian, aren't you?"

"No, really," Ronnie protested. "I'm not funny. All I can do is sneeze."

The kids laughed knowingly, amused that Ronnie still wasn't letting on to the gag.

"That'll be all then, thank you," said Ms. Scherer, waving Ronnie off the stage. She quickly jotted down a note on her pad. When Cindy peeked, she saw the words "Kid who sneezes. Funny timing. Deadpan. Maybe Cowardly Lion?"

Before calling out the next name, Ms. Scherer stood up from her seat in the auditorium and turned to face the students. "I've noticed," she said, "that everyone is doing a special skill—but no one is singing. How come no one is singing?"

Alexis raised her hand. "It's not easy to sing in front of people," she said. "Especially if you're shy."

"I never believe it when people tell me they're shy," said Ms. Scherer. "What's the point of being shy?"

"I'm not shy," Lizzie signed to Megan after they received Jann's translation.

"Me neither," Megan signed back.

"I'm singing!" cried Bethany. "Because I want to play Dorothy!"

Cindy tapped Megan's hand and signed, "Bethany says she wants to play Dorothy!" Megan's mouth fell open slightly but she didn't say a word. Even as Cindy was signing to Megan, three more girls called out, "Me too!"

"I want to play Dorothy!"

"I'm auditioning for Dorothy, Ms. Scherer!"

Cindy was signing as fast as she could. "And Lillian! And Trina! And Katherine!"

"Wow," signed Megan. "That's a lot of Dorothys!"

"Okay, then!" said Ms. Scherer. "Let's hear them!"

Bethany took the stage first and sang "Amazing Grace."

Megan elbowed Cindy. "What's she singing?" she asked.

"Some church song," said Cindy.

"And how is she?" asked Megan, somewhat urgently.

Cindy shrugged. She wagged her hand back and forth to indicate, "so-so."

Lillian was the next Dorothy to take the

stage. She took a deep breath and sang "Hush Little Baby," pausing every so often to take another deep breath and continue singing. She got as far as the part about the "billy goat" before Ms. Scherer cut her off with a brisk "Thank you!"

Megan nudged Cindy and gestured, "How was she?"

Cindy lowered her head and lifted her hand to pinch her nose as if she smelled something bad. "Stinko," she whispered.

Trina sang a song in Spanish, so Cindy didn't know the name of it. But when she was finished, Cindy raised a thumbs-up to let Megan know that she had done really well. "That girl can *sing*," she whispered, articulating with her lips so that Megan would understand.

Katherine's singing voice drew a quick thumbs-down from Cindy.

"What's she singing?" asked Lizzie.

"'Happy Birthday,'" said Cindy. She cocked her fingers toward her ears but didn't dare actually poke them inside so that anyone could see.

Even so, Megan elbowed Cindy and pointed toward the stage. "But look at her feet," Megan signed.

"What about them?" asked Cindy.

"She's really good with the *shoes*," said Megan. As she sang, Katherine twisted her ankles ever so slightly to show off her sneakers. It looked exactly like what Dorothy did in the movie with the ruby slippers. Cindy watched for a moment and turned toward Megan to acknowledge with a nod that what Megan had observed was true.

After the singing Dorothys had sung, Ms. Scherer went back to her roll call to pick another name at random. "Lizzie Rappaport!" she called. Naturally, Jann translated the name in full so that Lizzie knew she was "up." On top of that, Cindy turned to Lizzie and said, "Hey, Lizzie, you're up!"

However, as soon as Lizzie stepped into the aisle, Ms. Endee turned to whisper something to Ms. Scherer—and quickly rose from her chair. "Lizzie, I'm so sorry," said Ms. Endee. "This is your first day. We can't possibly expect you to have an audition prepared on your first day of school."

"No, really, it's okay. I'm ready!" Lizzie replied. Jann relayed the translation.

"Really?" said Ms. Endee. "I'm surprised."

"Megan told me this weekend that the class was holding auditions for *The Wizard of Oz*," Lizzie explained in sign language, "so I had time to prepare something."

"Oh!" said Ms. Endee, not entirely accustomed to students who fulfilled assignments without a lot of poking, prodding, and daily reminders.

"What are you going to do for us, Lizzie?" asked Ms. Scherer.

"I thought I'd *sing*," Lizzie signed. Jann translated on her behalf.

Megan and Cindy exchanged a look. "Lizzie's singing a song?" Cindy asked Megan.

"I don't know anything," said Megan. "She didn't say boo to me about it."

Lizzie arrived center stage and signed, "Hello, my name is Lizzie Rappaport."

"Hello, Lizzie," Ms. Scherer said in a warm, friendly voice.

"I just landed in the middle of this school," Lizzie continued, "which is kind of like Dorothy in *The Wizard of Oz*! So I thought that's the role I should try out for."

As Jann translated for Lizzie, Cindy turned toward Megan in shock. Clearly,

Megan was already in shock herself. Her mouth was slightly agape, and her eyes stared blankly at the stage.

Lizzie sought out Cindy in the third row and said, "Oh! Cindy! I forgot to ask. Will you help me?"

"Help you what?" Cindy replied.

"Sing the songs," said Lizzie. "You know them. I'm doing two songs we learned at summer camp!"

Oh, no! thought Megan.

"Sure!" said Cindy. "I'd be happy to help!" She crawled over Megan to reach the aisle, ran for the stage, and hopped over the lip to stand beside Lizzie.

"My first song is 'Let There Be Peace on Earth'!" said Lizzie. She nodded at Cindy—and Cindy began to sing, as Lizzie signed the words and swayed to the music.

Megan's jaw dropped. *Oh, no!* she thought. *Lizzie is going to ruin my whole audition!*

Megan watched the performance with her hands over her face, peeking between her fingers. Sure enough, it was all the moves they'd worked out together that summer. Lizzie did the song exactly the way she had done it with Megan. Megan thought she gave her own version a little more "oomph"—but she couldn't deny that it was the exact same song.

"That was *very* nice," said Ms. Scherer, when Lizzie stopped signing.

"I have another," said Lizzie.

"Let's hear it," said Ms. Scherer.

Megan watched as Lizzie turned to Cindy and signed, "Let's do 'She'll Be Coming Round the Mountain'!"

This is a nightmare! thought Megan. *Can this possibly get any worse?*

Of course, it made sense that Lizzie should have chosen the same two songs as Megan. They had spent two weeks working on the songs that summer. Even so, Megan couldn't believe that she and Lizzie had come up with the exact same audition— both in sign—and that Lizzie had been able to go first.

"That was *very* good, Lizzie!" said Ms. Scherer, leading the applause after Lizzie's rendition of "She'll Be Coming Round the Mountain." Lizzie wowed the audience. She was big, she was funny, she was interesting— she was new.

One boy in class called out, "Cool!"

Megan leaned forward to peek at Ms. Scherer's notepad and saw that she had written down the words "Potential Dorothy?"

Megan felt a sudden lump in her throat. Dorothy was the part that *she* wanted to play—and even though she was happy to have her friend Lizzie in her school, she didn't want Lizzie to have *everything*.

Cindy nudged Megan as she and Lizzie returned to the row. "Hey, Megan, move over," she said. Megan moved down a couple of seats so that girls could rejoin her in the row.

"Lizzie, that was *great*," Megan enthused. "You did really good!"

"Do you think so?" asked Lizzie. "I was really nervous."

"You didn't look nervous at all," said Megan. "Everybody loved it."

"Okay, kids," said Ms. Scherer, referring to her roll call. "Let me have your attention again. Next up, we have—let's see—Megan Merrill."

Megan flinched. Not only did she have to follow Lizzie—but she would be doing the same exact two songs—and doing them in sign language all over again. Everyone would think Megan was a total copycat!

Megan stood and headed for the stage—

trying to think of something, anything she could do instead of the two songs. Something that would convince Ms. Scherer that she was the one who should play Dorothy—that she would be perfect for the part.

And fortunately, just as Megan began to mount the steps to the stage, the lunch bell must have rung. When she turned to face the audience, all the kids were getting ready to leave the auditorium. Both Ms. Endee and Ms. Scherer were struggling to hold their attention. Megan quickly turned toward Jann to find out what was going on.

"The bell rang," Jann signed. "It's time for lunch. We ran out of time. We'll resume auditions tomorrow."

Whew! thought Megan. *"Saved by the bell!"*

She looked for Cindy and Lizzie among the seats. Several of her classmates had surrounded Lizzie, eager to introduce themselves and to get to know her better, now that they had seen her audition.

Everybody wants to meet the new Dorothy, thought Megan. *Only it's not me!*

TEN
COSTUME LADY

Hey, Mom! Remember *The Wizard of Oz*?" said Megan when she found her mother at her desk in the den that afternoon. Solo was tagging along beside her, waiting to be fed.

"Of course I do," said Lainee. "I've been waiting all day to hear how the auditions went."

"The auditions aren't over," said Megan. "Ms. Scherer—she's our drama teacher— she called my name to audition but then the bell rang."

"Oh, that's too bad," said Lainee. "So when do you get to audition?"

"I think tomorrow," said Megan. "And I thought you should know that I signed you up for the costume committee."

"What?" Lainee cried with alarm.

Megan couldn't imagine why she had to repeat the statement she had just made so clearly—but she did anyway, taking the time to spell out the word "costume" in case there was some misunderstanding. "I put your name down to make costumes for *The Wizard of Oz.*"

"I got it the first time," her mother responded. "I just couldn't *believe* it."

"What's the matter?" asked Megan. "Other kids' parents are getting involved. Why not you? Don't you love me?"

Lainee turned her chair away from the desk to face her daughter. "Megan," said her mother, "look at what you are wearing."

Megan studied her clothes. It was her customary school outfit of maybe-purple on sort-of-purple on arguably purple—Megan's usual look. "What about it?" said Megan.

"What part of that ensemble did I actually sew?" asked Lainee.

"None of it," Megan replied. "It all came from the store."

"*Exactly*!" said Lainee. "I don't know the first thing about *sewing*! I can't sew to save my life! Ask your father! If a button breaks on his shirt, he has to fix it himself because—ask him, he knows!—*I don't sew.* So there's absolutely no way I can put together costumes for your school show!"

"It's too late now," Megan protested. "I already signed you up for the committee."

"Well, if it's a committee," Lainee observed, "at least I'm not the only one."

"Actually, you were the only name on the list. Everyone else was signing up their moms and dads and I thought if I didn't, it would hurt my chance of being in the play!"

"Weren't there any other committees?" said her mother. "What about bake sale?"

"Full."

"What about box office?"

"Full."

"What about transportation?"

"Mom!" Megan cried. "Every list was already full except for costumes!"

"And do you know why that is?" her mother asked. "It's because nobody wants to do costumes!"

"Don't be mad, Mom," said Megan. "Ms. Endee and Ms. Scherer were so happy when I wrote down your name. Ms. Scherer said you were a lifesaver. She never said Lizzie's mom was a lifesaver for offering to run the box office."

"What does Lizzie's mom have to do with this?"

"Ugh!" cried Megan. She collapsed into a chair and sprawled dramatically, letting her limbs fling in all directions as though she was in agony.

"Okay," said her mother, "what happened at the audition today? Did Lizzie audition for Dorothy?"

"How did you know?" asked Megan.

"I'm a mind reader," said Lainee. Megan knew her mother was joking— although sometimes Megan suspected that maybe Lainee really could read minds.

"Lizzie auditioned for Dorothy and she sang both the songs that *I* was going to sing to audition for Dorothy! And right after she finished, I was called to audition—so I would have seemed like a total copycat because we would both have been singing the exact same thing!"

"But I thought you didn't audition today," her mother said.

"I *didn't*," Megan explained. "The bell rang and I escaped. But what am I going to do tomorrow? I can't memorize how to sign two new songs in one night! I'm going to show up with the exact same audition tomorrow!"

"Oh, dear," said Lainee.

"Five other girls want to play Dorothy, and even the ones who can't sing can all sing better than me!" Megan continued.

"Oh, dear," Lainee repeated.

Solo seemed to sense something was up because he barked twice and lay down at Megan's feet.

"And it gets worse," Megan continued. "Lizzie's mom showed up at the end of the school day and made a big deal about offering to volunteer for the show. Ms. Endee introduced her to Ms. Scherer and they were both all grateful, like 'Thank you, thank you, thank you.' So I had to do something!"

"So you volunteered me?" asked Lainee.

"Mom, I'm like the Marines! I see a problem and I take charge!"

It was a fairly perfect imitation of how Lainee had been when she had been upset about Solo, and it made Lainee smile. "Okay, okay," she said in defeat. "I guess I'm doing costumes!"

"No, you don't have to, Mom," said

Megan. "I'll tell Ms. Endee you can't do it. And I'll tell her I don't have anything prepared for my audition."

"But that's not true," said Lainee. "You worked so hard on your audition all weekend. I was so impressed with what you showed me after Lizzie and her mom left!"

"It's not going to impress Ms. Scherer after she already saw Lizzie do the same thing," said Megan.

"Megan," said Lainee, sitting beside her daughter on the arm of the chair. "You and Lizzie are similar. You're both deaf, yes—and you're both girls with a lot of personality. But the truth is that you're very different girls! I'm sure each of you brings something completely different to those songs. And I'm sure Ms. Scherer can see that. You're a very talented, outgoing girl—and you're not shy! How could she not cast you in the show?"

"I don't want to be a Munchkin!" said Megan, bursting into fake tears.

"Who said anything about being a Munchkin?"

"I already told everybody I want to be Dorothy," said Megan. "If I don't get to be Dorothy, I'll be so embarrassed."

"And what if Lizzie gets to be Dorothy?"

said Lainee. "How will you feel then?"

"Awful," said Megan. "And I'll feel awful that I feel awful because—I like Lizzie so much! And I'm happy she goes to my school! I'd be happy if she got to play Dorothy—but I wish it was back at her old school instead of mine."

"There's nothing wrong with wanting to play Dorothy," said Lainee, "but you have to deal with rejection. What happens if you don't get cast? You were so excited that Ms. Endee was going to do the play. You were so excited that Lizzie was going to be in your class. Is there a way you can be happy and excited about both things at once?"

"Just let me play Dorothy and I'll be happy," said Megan, with a very theatrical pout. She reached down to scratch Solo's head.

Her mother laughed. "What an actress!" she said. "Aw, honey—if you can put one ounce of that actress into your audition tomorrow, I'm sure Ms. Endee will give you the part."

"Do you think I'd be a good Dorothy?" Megan asked.

"You know I do," said Lainee. "I can see it now. You in pigtails with a basket and a little doggie." At that moment, Solo stood up and barked twice, rather loudly. "And speaking of little doggies," Lainee continued. "I know one who's hungry."

"It's Matt's turn to feed him," said Megan. "I bathe him and Matt walks him— and we take turns feeding him."

"Well, taking turns doesn't mean any- thing to a hungry dog," said Lainee. "Solo is hungry, and I think you should feed him."

"Okay," said Megan, with a trace of res- ignation. She hauled herself out of the chair and went to the kitchen.

Solo followed, watching intently as Megan walked across the kitchen to the broom closet where they stored the big bag of dog food. Megan turned to Solo and com- manded him to "stay"—then she picked the dog bowls off the linoleum and set them on the counter. She filled the water dish from the sink and carefully poured dog food from the sack into the food bowl. She had to be careful because the bag was still pretty heavy. If she wasn't careful, she could lose her grip and end up with dog food all over the floor. The whole time, Solo waited, as Megan had instructed him to do, watching as she prepared the bowls.

Megan set the bowls on the linoleum and started to leave the kitchen—almost forgetting that she hadn't told Solo it was okay to eat. She turned around and saw that Solo was still sitting in the same spot.

"Good boy!" Megan said, scratching his neck affectionately. "Good boy!"

Solo kept his eyes on Megan, waiting for the sign that it was okay to eat.

"Go ahead," said Megan, nodding toward the dog bowls. "Chow down."

Solo sprang forward and huddled close to the bowls as he ate his dinner. Megan looked up to see that Matt had entered the kitchen. "What are you doing here?" asked Megan. "I thought you had softball practice."

"Rain," said Matt, as though that explained everything. "Hey, what are you doing? I was going to feed the dog."

"He was hungry," Megan explained, "so Mom told me to go ahead and feed him."

"Don't mess me up, Megan," said Matt. "I promised Solo I'd feed him today 'cause I'm not going to see him tomorrow because of softball practice. You're always messing me up!"

"He was hungry and I fed him," Megan

snapped. "Next time he's hungry—I'm going to tell Mom you won't let me feed him."

Matt grabbed an apple off the counter. "What's your problem?" he said before the first big bite.

"I'm sick of hearing about your softball practice," said Megan. "I got things to worry about too. You knew my audition was today, and you didn't even bother to ask me how it went!"

"Okay," said Matt, still chewing. "How'd the audition go today?"

"It's tomorrow," said Megan. "They ran out of time."

"Good luck tomorrow," said Matt, heading back upstairs—but Megan blocked his path. "Matt, do you see me as Dorothy?" she asked.

"No, I see you as Megan," said Matt.

"Don't be stupid," said Megan. "You know what I'm saying. In *The Wizard of Oz*, would you see me as Dorothy? Mom says she does, but that's just because she loves me. I figured you would tell me the truth."

"Maybe if you had a dog," said Matt. "And a Scarecrow and a Tin Man and a Cowardly Lion."

"Don't be stupid, Matt," said Megan.

"It doesn't matter if I see you as Dorothy or Mom sees you as Dorothy," said Matt. "What matters is whether whoever's picking the parts sees you as Dorothy."

"That's Ms. Scherer," said Megan. "And Ms. Endee."

"Then you should worry about what they think," said Matt. "Maybe you should ride in on a tornado or something. That way she'd definitely see you as Dorothy. Hey! It's too bad we don't know a Scarecrow or a Tin Man or a Cowardly Lion."

"Don't be stupid, Matt," said Megan. "I'm serious."

"I sort of *was* being serious," said Matt. "You fed him, right?" Matt was pointing at the dog.

"Yes, I told you, I fed him," said Megan.

"Okay," Matt replied. "Leave him with me. We're working on the meaning of 'no.'"

When Megan left the kitchen, Matt was pointing to the kitchen counter and signing and saying to Solo, "No! No! No!" Solo was watching intently but it was anybody's guess whether he had the least idea as to what Matt meant.

*

When Megan went to bed that night, she still had no idea how to make Ms. Endee and Ms. Scherer see her as Dorothy when she auditioned the next day. It was too late to learn two new songs. And she didn't want to come in with some ordinary special skill, like using sign language or winning a stare-down contest. She pulled the blankets close and called, "Solo!"

A few moments later, the door inched open and the dog arrived in the room. He crawled onto the bed and curled up at Megan's feet. Lainee appeared in the door-way as well. "Ready for bed, Dorothy?" she asked.

"Don't call me that," said Megan. "I still don't know what I'm going to do tomor-row."

"Just do your best," said Lainee. "Sweet dreams. Sleep tight."

"Good night, Mom," said Megan.

And Lainee switched out the light.

When Megan woke up in the middle of the night to use the bathroom, she threw back the blankets and headed for the door. Solo rustled from the foot of the bed and fol-lowed her into the hall. Megan closed the bathroom door, so Solo had to wait by himself in the hall. But when Megan opened the door again, Solo was still waiting.

Megan walked back down the hall and into her room, with Solo trailing behind. She crawled onto her bed and pulled the comforter around her. Then Solo hopped onto the bed to curl up at her feet once more.

"Good boy," said Megan, already half-asleep, without a second thought.

When Megan opened her eyes the next morning, the sunlight landed right in her eyes and made her squint. The very first thing that occurred to her was that she still didn't know how to make her audition "special and different" that day.

She had only a few minutes before her father would step into the bedroom and tug her big toe—their usual signal for "time to get up." She didn't imagine she was going to have a brilliant idea between the first stretch of the day and the time it took for her dad to tug her big toe.

Megan sighed and rolled over, wishing she could just hug her pillow and go back to sleep. But when she did, she found that she was nose-to-nose—nose-to-cold-wet-nose—with Solo. The dog had crawled from the foot of the bed to the top of the bed in the course of the night and was asleep on the pillow beside her. Megan smiled to think that her dog had been beside her throughout the night. Solo was still sound asleep and breathing softly. His mouth was slightly open, and his tongue was hanging out so that it looked as if he was smiling.

What a good dog, thought Megan. *I am so lucky. I have the best dog in the—*

And that was when Megan had the most incredible, the most brilliant, the most positively perfect idea.

ELEVEN
ONE GOOD TRICK

The next day, the students returned to the auditorium for four more auditions. Megan, Cindy, Stuart Masters, and Mickey Basu.

"Who did we leave off with?" asked Ms. Scherer, sitting beside Ms. Endee in the first row.

"Megan!" cried Alexis. "Megan is next."

"Yes, that's right, of course," said Ms. Scherer. "Megan, you're up!"

Jann signed the translation to Megan—but Megan was already out of her seat, edging toward the aisle. She gestured rapidly for one moment—and ran up the aisle and out of the auditorium.

"Where did she go?" asked Ms. Scherer.

Jann shrugged. Ms. Endee shrugged.

"Where did she go?" Ms. Scherer repeated to the students—but nobody seemed to know. "I hope we didn't scare her away." The students laughed good-naturedly.

A moment later, Megan returned through the doors—but this time, she appeared to be leading something—on a *leash*. As she drew closer to the stage, the students could see that it was a dog.

In fact, it was Solo.

Megan ran with the dog trotting just behind her heels. They jumped up the stairs and onto the stage. When she looked into the audience, she noticed Bethany, Lillian, Trina, and Katherine staring at her with their mouths wide open and their arms crossed. Lizzie leaned forward and smiled. Clearly, another Dorothy had entered the race.

"What have we here?" said Ms. Scherer at the sight of Megan with a very real and rather large dog at her side.

"This is Solo," said Megan. "He's my dog."

"I see," said Ms. Scherer. "Hello, Solo. Well, Megan, it's clear to see which part you're trying out for, isn't it?"

"I planned to sing," Megan explained,

"but my songs are the exact same two songs that Lizzie did yesterday because we both learned them at summer camp. So then I thought I'd do a special skill instead—because I didn't want people to think I was being a copycat. And my skill is dog tricks!"

The children laughed.

"Wait," Megan explained. "Not me doing dog tricks. The dog doing dog tricks. Solo does them but I call out the commands." Solo barked as if in agreement with the explanation. "And then I figured," Megan continued, "that I could sing the songs and do the dog tricks together."

"Well, let's see it," said Ms. Scherer.

"Cindy!" Megan cried over the edge of the stage. "I need you to sing the songs again!"

"Sure thing," said Cindy, leaping from her seat and heading for the stage.

"Well, I certainly know how well Cindy can sing," said Ms. Scherer, "because I've already heard her sing so many times!" The kids had a good chuckle, and when they stopped laughing, Cindy was onstage—a few steps away from Megan and Solo.

Megan turned to Solo and commanded

him to "sit down" and "stay"—and then she nodded at Cindy.

"Which one first?" said Cindy.

"Let There Be Peace on Earth," said Megan.

"You got it," said Cindy.

Megan counted, "One, two, ready, begin," and Cindy started to sing. As she did, Megan went into her version of the song with sign language.

Something about performing in front of other people brought out the very best in Megan. Her face lit up in a certain way. She drew out the gestures of the sign language in a way that seemed to make the meaning more obvious—the same way she had explained the obviousness of sign language to Tony in the playground. She might have had Cindy singing behind her and Solo sitting beside her—but when Megan was performing, it was difficult to notice anyone else onstage. Megan was completely comfortable in front of an audience. In fact, there was no place else she would rather be. And she let the audience know it. At the end of Megan's song, her classmates gave her a hearty round of applause.

"Megan, that was wonderful," said Ms.

Scherer, "but I thought you were going to do dog tricks while you sang."

"I did," said Megan, pointing at Solo. "I told him to sit down and stay. And he sat down and stayed. You don't know how hard that is!"

Megan's remark drew a big laugh from the crowd—especially from Jann and Ms. Endee. "Yes, I certainly do," said Ms. Endee. "I face a classroom of students every day. I wish it was as easy as 'sit!' and 'stay!'"

"I have another song," said Megan. "And Solo knows more tricks."

"Let's hear it," said Ms. Scherer. "This should be fun."

"Okay, here we go," said Megan.

She reached into her pocket and pulled out a dog bone. Solo leaped to his feet at the first whiff of the treat—but Megan raised a finger firmly, intending to hold him in his place. She nodded at Cindy who began to sing "She'll Be Coming Round the Mountain." Megan used her sign language and movement to capture the spirit of the song—and at the end of every phrase, she lifted the dog bone over Solo's head so that he would jump into the air and bark, right in time with the music. It was raucous and rambunctious and a whole lot of fun.

If Ms. Scherer was looking for students to show two completely different sides of themselves onstage, Megan had done it. Because she was sensitive and real during the first song—and silly and playful during the second.

Megan couldn't know if her audition was good enough for her to be cast as Dorothy—but she couldn't have had a better time. As Megan led Solo off the stage, her classmates applauded and several gathered near her to pet him.

"Thank you, Megan," said Ms. Scherer.

"Thank you, Ms. Scherer," said Megan.

"No, thank *you*," said Ms. Scherer. "And thank you, Solo, too. Now what happens to the dog?"

"Don't worry," said Megan. "My mom is waiting in the parking lot. She's been sitting in her car."

"Excellent," said Ms. Endee. "It was fun to have Solo visit—but we don't want to turn the classroom into 'Mary Had a Little Lamb.' Cindy, would you accompany Megan and Solo to the parking lot—and then come right back, because you still have to audition!"

"Yes, ma'am," said Cindy.

She hopped off the stage to join Megan—and both girls ran up the aisle with the dog.

"It went great, Mom," said Megan, as they loaded Solo into the car. "Thanks so much for waiting and letting me bring Solo as a surprise."

"That's what mothers are for," said Lainee. "You and Cindy had better get back to class."

"Yes, ma'am," said Cindy. The girls stepped onto the curb and waved as Megan's mother drove out of the parking lot.

"You really did great," said Cindy. "That was so much fun watching you sing with the dog."

"I only did it so I could get Ms. Scherer to see me as Dorothy," said Megan, "and why not? I've got my own Toto!"

"He's a big Toto," said Cindy, "but I think it did the trick. I heard kids saying how great you would be as Dorothy."

"I kind of feel bad though," said Megan. "I know Bethany and Trina and Katherine and Lillian want to be Dorothy too."

"And I think Keisha also wants to be Dorothy," said Cindy.

"Keisha?" asked Megan. "Really?"

"Didn't you notice she's been wearing her hair in braids to school?" said Cindy.

"Oh, and Lizzie wants to be Dorothy too!" said Megan. "It's not much fun being up against a friend."

"What are you talking about?" said Cindy. "Lizzie doesn't want to be Dorothy!"

"Yes, she does," said Megan.

"No, she doesn't," said Cindy. "Have you asked her? Because last time I talked to Lizzie she said 'no way' does she want to play Dorothy."

"She said so onstage during her audition!" said Megan. "And she said so when she was at my house!"

"Well, I don't know about that," said Cindy. "All I know is what she told me yesterday afternoon."

They got back to the auditorium in time to see Mickey Basu juggling oranges and singing "Three Blind Mice." Megan wanted to ask Lizzie if it was true about not wanting to be Dorothy—but between Mickey Basu's wrong notes and the commotion over the runaway oranges, she couldn't get Lizzie's attention.

After that, it was time for Cindy's

audition and Megan gave her full attention to her friend.

Cindy reached center stage and introduced herself. "Hi, my name is Cindy," she said, "and since you've already heard me sing, I thought I'd do a trick instead." Cindy reached for a glass of water perched on a stool and continued. "I will now drink this glass of water while reciting all fifty states in alphabetical order." She raised the glass to her lips and began to drink. As she did, she raised her other hand and began to sign, using the finger alphabet.

A L A B A M A ,

A L A S K A ,

A R I Z O N A ,

A R K A N S A S

"It doesn't make sense to me," said Casey over lunch. "Megan's audition was great and all, but in the book, Dorothy is a girl who can hear and talk—and Toto is a little dog. So I'm sorry—but I just don't see a Dorothy who's deaf and talks with her hands and has a great big dog for Toto!"

Casey hadn't seen Megan approaching from behind with her lunch tray. She was more than a little surprised when Megan sat down beside her just as she finished her little rant about a deaf Dorothy. Alexis and Cindy were already sitting at the round table on the patio with Casey.

"It doesn't make any difference," Cindy argued.

"What are you guys talking about?" asked Megan.

Cindy signed the word "nothing" as Alexis leaped to Megan's defense.

"Nice attitude, Casey!" Alexis responded. "You could end up being the Tin Woodman 'cause you wear braces. Everybody in the audience knows the play's only pretend—so what does it matter?"

"What's going on?" Megan asked Cindy. She had been able to read Alexis's lips so she had had some idea that they were talking about her before she had reached the table.

"It doesn't matter," Cindy responded in

sign to Megan. "Except the Tin Woodman here was being a little stupid, and Alexis gave it to her good."

"What?" said Megan.

"Nothing," said Cindy. "I'll tell you later."

"Has anybody seen Lizzie?" said Megan. "I really need to talk to her."

"Your little deaf friend is in the bathroom," said Casey.

Megan could read Casey's lips—so she knew exactly what Casey had just said—but she wasn't exactly sure about the tone, so she couldn't be absolutely sure if Casey was being nice or mean. So she went ahead and asked, "Are you being nice or are you being mean?"

Casey acted surprised. "I'm being nice," she said—even though that was a lie.

"No, you're not," said Megan, shaking her head "no" with confidence. "When I ask people, 'Are you being nice or are you being mean?' and they act *apologetic*—then I know they were being nice. But if they act all *surprised*—like you just did?—then I know they were being mean."

"She *was* being mean," said Alexis. "Not super-mean, but yes, nasty."

Casey picked up her tray with a little huff. "I'm leaving you guys alone," she said.

"Fine," said Alexis. "Go hang out with the Munchkins."

"I guess I was right, then," said Megan, as they watched Casey leave the table. "She was being mean. What's her problem?"

"She's crabby about the auditions because everybody keeps telling her she'd make a great Tin Woodman," said Alexis.

"I think maybe her braces are too tight," said Cindy. "That's why she's so crabby all the time." Megan and Alexis looked at each other, and their eyes widened in surprise. Cindy almost never said anything the least bit mean about somebody else. This was quite a shocking remark. And then they started laughing.

Once they were finished, Megan asked, "So when do you think Ms. Scherer is putting up the list?"

"I don't know, Megan," Cindy replied. "Ask Ms. Endee."

"I'm afraid to ask," said Megan. "I don't want to annoy her. I just want to know who got what."

"The anticipation is killing me!" cried Cindy. "I'm about to burst!"

Megan squared off. "So," she began, "who was better? Bethany, Trina, Katherine, Lillian—or *Keisha*—or *Lizzie*—or me?"

"It doesn't matter what I think," said Cindy. "You know I'd love to see you play Dorothy! But who knows what Ms. Scherer is thinking!"

"My palms are sweaty," said Megan. "I must be nervous just thinking about the auditions because my palms are sweaty."

"I'm glad I don't have my hopes set on Dorothy," said Cindy. "Ms. Scherer could cast me as a Munchkin, a Monkey—or even Auntie Em—and I'd still be happy. But if she doesn't cast you as Dorothy, you're going to feel awful, and I'm going to feel awful for you."

"Thanks, but you're not making me feel better right now," said Megan, slightly exasperated. "I'm nervous enough!"

"Do you want me to ask Ms. Endee when she's putting up the list?"

"No!" said Megan. "I just want to know the names on it."

At that moment, Megan saw Lizzie approaching them from across the patio. "There's Lizzie," she said. "I've been looking for her." She got up from the table and ran to talk to her friend.

"Lizzie," she said, just a bit breathless from the run, "I wanted to talk to you about

something before we sat down with everybody else."

"What's up?" said Lizzie.

"I'm sorry it's been so weird that we're
both auditioning for *Wizard!*," said Megan.

"What's 'so weird'?"

"I mean, that we're both the deaf girls in
class and we're both up for Dorothy and
we're still friends, but it makes it weird
being friends," said Megan.

Lizzie laughed. "Megan!" she said. "We
put on plays at my old school all the time.
And since everybody was deaf, deaf kids
were always auditioning against deaf kids. It
was no big deal! I'm brand-new at this
school—and there are so many girls who
want to be Dorothy. I never expected to get
the part. And I certainly won't be mad if I
don't."

"Are you sure?" asked Megan. "Because
I know how much your mom wants you to
be Dorothy."

"Of course my mom does," Lizzie
replied, "but that's not me."

"Lizzie," said Megan. "You don't have to
pretend you don't want to play Dorothy just
to make me feel better."

"I'm serious!" said Lizzie. "I was Alice in

Alice in Wonderland at my school last year—so I'm okay playing one of the other characters in *The Wizard of Oz*. In fact, if you really want to know, I've got my heart set on the Good Witch—'cause that way I get the tiara, the big puffy dress, and maybe a big entrance."

Megan laughed because Lizzie was already parading around the patio as if she was floating into the scene inside a great big bubble.

"Watch what happens," said Megan. "With our luck, we'll both get cast as Munchkins, and that's all. What do you bet we get cast as Munchkins?"

"Wouldn't that be perfect?" said Lizzie, nudging her shoulder into her friend's. She pointed to herself—and then to Megan. "We'll be Munchkin #1—and Munchkin #2!"

Cindy interrupted their laughter by charging between them and grabbing their hands. "You guys!" she cried. "Hurry up! Come on, come on!"

"What's the matter?" said Megan. "Where are you taking us?"

"The cast list is up!" Cindy exclaimed. "Come on! Ms. Endee posted the cast!"

TWELVE
HAPPY ENDINGS

Life doesn't always have happy endings. A kid can want something a whole lot—like a trampoline or a pony or a new bike—and then not get it. A girl could have a great day at school and come home to sad news about her grandmother or grandfather. A boy can have a long run of bad luck—flunk a test, miss his ride home, bust his skateboard, scab his knee, and rip his brand-new jeans. Nothing is fair, life stinks, and it simply couldn't get worse.

So the bad news was—Cindy didn't get cast as the Wicked Witch of the West, the role she really wanted though she didn't dare tell anyone. Donny Vargas didn't get cast as the Wizard, even though he had already told his parents that he had been.

Frankie Adams didn't get chosen to be the Scarecrow, despite the fact that he'd already memorized five lines of Scarecrow dialogue. Casey Waite would play the Tin Woodman, a casting decision that everyone thought was perfect, except for Casey. And Keisha Dunbar cried herself to sleep that night because she didn't get cast as Dorothy even after wearing pigtails to school for two days in a row—for *nothing*.

But there was good news. Much to his surprise, Tony Rosenblum was cast as the Wizard after convincing himself that he would never get picked. Ronnie Jiu was cast as the Cowardly Lion. Alexis was chosen to play several parts, including Auntie Em and the Tree That Throws Apples, which made her very happy. Keisha Dunbar was cast as the Scarecrow which, she had to admit, was still a great part. Tracy Benz was cast as the Wicked Witch—which everybody figured was because she'd been so scary on her roller skates and scary in a different way with the karate. Much to her delight, Lizzie was cast as the Good Witch of the North. And sure enough, Megan was cast as Dorothy. The cast list even had an entry that read, "Toto: Solo!"

Apart from that, every kid who wanted to be a Munchkin was one, and every kid who wanted to be a Winged Monkey was one too. Cindy was cast as both Munchkin and Monkey, so she had plenty to help her to get over the disappointment about the Wicked Witch.

The same afternoon that the cast list was posted, Ms. Scherer explained that she had put together a rough draft of a script, loosely based on the book, student's ideas, and classroom suggestions. This version of the script was already being rewritten by a committee of student writers that included Alexis, Bethany, Donny Vargas, and Tony Rosenblum.

"Rehearsals start tomorrow afternoon!" Ms. Scherer announced. "So make sure you get those permission slips signed by your parents! I expect you to be on time and I expect you to be prepared. We've got a lot of work to do, people, but we're also going to have a lot of fun. So let's get cracking!"

Alexis's hand was raised in the air throughout Ms. Scherer's speech. "Yes?" said Ms. Scherer, pointing to Alexis.

"But Ms. Scherer," Alexis asked, "with all the work we have to do on the play, when are we supposed to do our homework?"

"That's the trick," said Ms. Scherer. "You have to find the time to attend rehearsal and still do your homework—because your schoolwork is still your priority here."

"And I'm not handing out *less* homework just because we're doing a play," said Ms. Endee. When all the kids groaned, Ms. Endee added, "I will—however—see if I can find chunks of time during the day for you to catch up on your homework in class. But you have to promise to be disciplined about it!"

Cindy turned to Megan and signed, "This is huge! They expect us to do a lot of work!"

Megan smiled but didn't sign anything back. She agreed that it sounded like a lot of work—and a lot of responsibility. On top of all the work that had to go into the play and into homework, Megan also had to keep working with Solo to make sure he was ready for the play. But Megan wasn't complaining about anything since she'd been lucky enough to land the role of Dorothy.

The role of Dorothy was actually sort of double-cast—with Bethany listed as "the spoken Dorothy." Ms. Scherer's idea was that Megan would play Dorothy onstage—

and that Bethany would sing and speak the role from a chair positioned on the side of the stage. When Megan asked what that meant, Ms. Endee explained, "The way Jann helps you in the classroom, Bethany will help the audience from the stage."

"But I'm Dorothy, right?" asked Megan before she left the classroom that afternoon.

"Yes, you're Dorothy," said Ms. Scherer. "And Solo is Toto."

"Great!" Megan replied. "This is going to be so much fun!"

"But Megan," Ms. Scherer added, "Solo does know a few more tricks, doesn't he? I mean, it would be nice if we could get him to do something more than just sit and stay and bark."

"Oh, he knows *tons* of tricks," said Megan. "He's always doing tricks! We have to make him stop at night and go to bed, otherwise he'd keep us up doing tricks!"

Before Megan shared the good news about *Wizard!* with her mom and dad, she tracked down her brother, Matt, in his bedroom.

"Matt, it's an emergency," she said.

Matt sprawled across his bed with a GameBoy, seemingly unimpressed by Megan's sense of urgency. He lifted his face so that Megan could read his lips but he kept his focus on the GameBoy. "The sign on the door says, 'keep out.'"

"Yes, but that doesn't mean *me*," Megan replied.

"Yes, it does," Matt insisted.

"Well, it's a stupid rule," said Megan. "And you'd want me to break the rule if it was an emergency—and this is!"

"Is the house on fire?" asked Matt.

"No," said Megan.

"A tornado?"

"No," said Megan. By this point, she was wagging her head like a dog, saying no to anything that Matt said.

"Unless Mom found another dead lizard in the pantry, it's not such an emergency!" said Matt.

"Matt! Let me speak!" said Megan. "We have to train Solo. We have to teach him a lot more dog tricks!"

"You taught him tricks before," said Matt. "You teach him."

"He has to learn a whole lot of great tricks really fast, and I'm not going to have the time to do it all by myself!" Megan insisted.

"And how does this situation qualify as an emergency?" asked Matt, suddenly suspicious.

"Because I need to know you'll help!" said Megan. "I got cast as Dorothy in *Wizard!*—and Solo was cast as Toto. But Ms. Scherer thinks Solo knows a lot more tricks than he actually does! She thinks he can roll over and shake hands and jump through a hoop!"

"Why does she think that?"

"Because I told her!"

"So you lied," said Matt, pointing an accusatory finger.

"I didn't lie!" Megan protested. "I wanted the part! And I knew that you could help me do it! Help me out, Matt! It's so easy when you know sign language because Solo knows sign language, too! You could teach Solo to do *anything*! He could make your bed and pick up your clothes and clean your room!" Megan flung her hands about Matt's always less-than-tidy room.

Matt slumped back on the bed and considered his sister. "You really think Solo might make my bed?" he asked.

Megan smirked. "I know we can train Solo!" she said, half-kidding as well. "Say yes, say yes, say yes!"

"But what's in it for me?" said Matt. "Why should I help you train the dog? I'm not playing Dorothy. I'm not even in your stupid play."

"A clean room, Matt," said Megan, all helpless and pathetic. "Come on! Who else can I ask? You already know sign language! Trust me—I taught him to sit and stay and bark. But I need your help with everything else."

"Oh, all right," said Matt.

"Thanks!" said Megan, brightening immediately. She grabbed her brother's arm and tugged. "Come on, let's get started right now!"

It was too soon to have another world-famous lasagna to celebrate the news that Megan had been cast as Dorothy in *The Wizard of Oz*. All the same, Lainee wanted to do something special. She reached into the top cabinet and retrieved the one red china dinner plate. It was something David and Lainee had done when the kids were little, to reward a good report card or a trophy in the playground soccer league. When the family sat down to the table that night, everyone had ordinary white dinner plates—but Megan had her meatloaf, mashed potatoes, and brussels sprouts on a shiny red plate.

"—and then Ms. Scherer told me that Solo was cast as 'your little dog Toto too!'"

Megan explained, finishing the story for about the eighth time that night. So far, she had shared the news with: her family, of course; her friends in other grades in the playground; the bus driver on the way home; their backyard neighbors, the Ortegas; her grandmother on her father's side, her grandfather on her mother's side; and the special-delivery guy who showed up on their doorstep with a package for her dad. Good news can be exhausting.

"Does Solo have to go to every rehearsal?" said David.

"No, Dad!" said Megan. "I do, of course, because Dorothy is in almost every scene and I have so much to learn! But Ms. Scherer said we should only bring Solo in a couple of times and then during dress rehearsals and the shows."

"Omigosh," said Lainee. "*Dress* rehearsal! I was so happy about the news that you'd been cast as Dorothy that I forgot all about the *costume* committee."

"What costume committee?" asked David.

Matt offered the explanation. "Megan signed Mom up for the costume committee without asking her permission first."

"You?" David said to Lainee. He held his hand over his mouth and snickered quietly for several moments.

"See, Megan?" said her mother. "I told you it was funny."

"I'm sorry to laugh, honey," said David, "but you've got lots of help, right?"

"Ask Megan," said Lainee.

"She's the only one on the committee," Megan answered.

David resumed his snickering, hiding behind his hand. "I'm sorry to disappoint you, Megan—but your mother can't sew," he said.

"So I found out," said Megan.

"But seriously," David said to Lainee, "you don't have to make *all* the costumes for *all* the kids—*all* by yourself, right? Tell me I'm wrong! Somebody's got to help, right?"

Lainee was silent. She skewered a brussels sprout on her plate, put it in her mouth—and began to chew.

Suddenly, Megan got loud. "Are our costumes going to be awful?" she demanded. "Because I don't want ugly costumes! You have to promise, Mom. You have to promise we're going to have good costumes!"

"They'll be *fine*, honey," said Lainee.

"They'll be *wonderful*. You'll see. I'm sure I'll be able to recruit some other moms who sew—if I can find any who know how to sew."

"You know what I'd do?" said David, working on a mouthful of meatloaf. "I'd go to a thrift shop and pick up a bunch of old pillowcases. Cut two holes for the arms; cut a hole for the head. Paint or dye the pillowcases. And you've got little tunics for the Munchkins."

Lainee aimed her fork down the table at her husband. "Now *that* is a really good idea," she said. "I could hand out the pillowcases and have the children paint them themselves."

"You could even get them to paint yellow bricks on the back side of the pillowcases," David continued, "so that when the Munchkins turn around—presto!—instant Yellow Brick Road."

"David!" said Lainee. "You're a lifesaver!"

"Great idea, Dad!" said Megan. "How'd you come up with that?"

"I wasn't in college skits for nothing," her father replied matter of fact. "I was quite the clown in college."

"Maybe I should have signed up Dad for the committee," said Megan.

"Yes!" said Lainee. "Take my name off, and sign up your father."

"No!" said David. "I work plenty hard enough as it is. You can just keep me on as your mother's 'consultant.'"

"Okay, Dad," said Megan.

"And instead of actually *sewing*, you can hot-glue the costumes together," said David, still brimming with good ideas. "I've got a hot-glue gun in the garage."

"Thanks, dear," said Lainee.

"And there's a box of those orange scrunchy things you use to scrub pots and pans," he continued. "You could use those to make the Cowardly Lion."

"Orange scrunchy things?" said Lainee. "You think so? Instead of orange yarn?"

"Yarn will just hang there," said David. "You won't get the same kind of bounce you get with scrubbing pads."

Matt and Megan exchanged sideways smiles—clearly impressed and delighted with their dad's unlikely interest in the costumes.

"And it sounds crazy," David went on, "but you could make the witches' costumes out of garbage bags."

"Dad!" Megan protested. "I don't want a dress made out of a garbage bag!"

"You're Dorothy," said David. "We'll put you in a dress. But you're going to need shoes. Ruby slippers, right?"

"Ruby slippers are the whole point, Dad!" said Megan. "They're the reason why the Wicked Witch is so mad!"

"One pair of ruby slippers," said David, making a mental note. "Maybe spray paint? And glitter?"

"But in the book, they're not ruby slippers," said Megan. "And technically, we're doing the book, not the movie. In the book, they're silver slippers—so we should probably make them silver instead of red."

"Can't we make them more fun than silver?" asked David. "I know you like purple so much."

"Dad!" said Megan, delighted. "Purple?!"

"I was thinking *your* Dorothy would probably prefer purple slippers. So maybe purple slippers instead of ruby."

"Sapphire slippers! Dad's a genius!" Megan enthused. "Mom, are you writing this down?"

THIRTEEN
FRENCH FRIES

Rehearsals were fun before they became work.

Ms. Scherer had the students read the first draft of the *Wizard!* script out loud in class, assigning all the roles so that everyone knew who said what. The rewrite committee sat on the side of the room with pencils, taking notes when the script needed help. "It's a chance to just throw it all out there and see what we've got," said Ms. Scherer. "Then we'll break it down scene by scene and get to work!"

After that, rehearsals took place after school and on the weekends, unless Ms. Endee managed to squeeze in a little rehearsal during class time. Some days she reserved the gym and took an hour to

review the polka. Of course, instead of simply
reviewing the dance, the students figured
out how the Munchkins would polka when
Dorothy's house landed on the Wicked
Witch. It was pretty much the same way the
students polkaed, except that Munchkins
laughed in high-pitched giggles. Rehearsals
were a little chaotic, of course, but they
helped to set traffic patterns so that no
Munchkin got knocked over. They also
helped "to keep the polka fresh!" as Ms.
Endee liked to say.

A schedule was posted for the after-
school rehearsals so that kids had to attend
only on the days when they were actually in
the scene being staged. As Dorothy, of
course, Megan was pretty much stuck in
rehearsal from day 1. When Dorothy connected with the Scarecrow, the Tin
Woodman, and the Cowardly Lion, a regu-
lar group began to develop—which made
certain things easier, like car pools, for
example.

Ms. Scherer tried to schedule the big
scenes—like the ones with the tornado, the
Munchkins, the Monkeys, and the big good-
bye scene at the end—on Tuesdays so that
the students would have plenty of time to

rehearse the scenes over and over during the week.

The Hot Dog Joint was a small restaurant across the street from the school auditorium. It was scarcely bigger than the storefront window that advertised its name. A few tables were positioned on a covered patio with a yellow-and-red awning. At one end was a countertop, five stools, and not much else. A small blackboard was positioned between squeeze bottles of ketchup and mustard on the counter. The menu was basically hot dogs, turkey dogs, soft drinks, and a bucket of French fries—either smothered in hot melted cheese or not.

At the end of rehearsal, Megan and the other Leading Ladies got permission from Ms. Endee to hang out at the Hot Dog Joint while they waited for their rides home. Ms. Endee said it was okay "as long as you convince Jann to keep an eye on you." Jann agreed to sit at a nearby table with a book so that the girls were properly chaperoned.

"And it would be nice if you brought me an order of French fries from time to time," Ms. Scherer interjected over her clipboard. "With cheese, please."

"You know about the cheese fries?" asked Megan.

Ms. Scherer looked at Megan and smiled. "That Hot Dog Joint has the best cheese fries in town," she said.

And so it was, that every day after rehearsal, the girls were able to go through a bucket of fries smothered in cheese at the Hot Dog Joint. It was the perfect snack to share—salty but sweet, gooey but fun to eat, and *lots of it*.

"I wonder where my mom is," said Megan, searching the street for a glimpse of her mother's car. "These days are so crazy. I get home from rehearsal, and I still have to do my homework and I still have to take care of Solo. Tonight I was hoping to teach Solo a brand-new trick!"

"What trick?" asked Cindy.

"You should teach Solo how to do your homework," said Lizzie—and everybody laughed after Cindy translated the joke.

"Let me see your face," said Megan, waving the French fry in her hand as though it was a cigarette. It was a spot-on imitation of Mrs. Lopez, Enrique's mom, who had volunteered to do their makeup backstage. The girls knew that Mrs. Lopez smoked cigarettes outside the auditorium during breaks. Cindy had seen her light a cigarette one time—and of course, Megan noticed the smell of cigarettes anytime Mrs. Lopez came near. Megan's imitation of Mrs. Lopez smoking a cigarette was just about perfect. "You look so pale!" Megan continued. "We need color on you! Lots of color!" She waved her hand in Lizzie's face, pausing to pinch Lizzie's cheeks. She pretended to puff on the French fry and went on a wild coughing jag, fanning the air to get rid of make-believe smoke.

The girls laughed wildly.

"I like Mrs. Lopez and all," said Cindy. "She's super-nice—and so is Enrique. But I wish Mrs. Lopez wouldn't smoke all the time!"

"Her fingers smell so awful!" said Megan. "And they're always in your face!"

"I didn't notice her smelly fingers," said Alexis.

"I notice smell more because I'm deaf," said Megan. "Ask Lizzie. She noticed it too. You can't not!"

"Cigarettes stink," said Lizzie, pinching her nose.

"I heard that Mrs. Lopez used to be an actress," said Alexis.

"Really?" said Megan, her curiosity tweaked. "How do you know that?"

"Because I asked her if it was true," said Alexis, "and she told me. She said, before she got married, she used to be an actress."

"What kind of actress?" asked Lizzie.

"Apparently a pretty good one," said Alexis. "She said she won awards."

"What kind of awards?"

"I don't know," said Alexis. "Ask her yourself."

"Maybe I will," said Megan. "Maybe she was a movie star. You can tell she was really beautiful."

"How can you tell that?" asked Cindy.

"Her green eyes," said Megan. "Haven't you noticed? And her long, thick eyelashes. And she has really pretty hair."

"I thought you only noticed she was stinky," said Cindy, taking a handful of French fries and twitching them in Megan's face as if they were Mrs. Lopez's fingers. "I'll get you, my pretty!"

"Cindy," said Megan, "sometimes I think there's a Wicked Witch inside of you, just waiting to get out!"

*

"Can I sit with you guys?"

Keisha Dundar stood next to their table. She was wearing her normal clothes but still wore the straw hat she used in the play.

"Sure, Keisha," said Megan. "We always have room for the Scarecrow!"

"I was waiting for my mom," said Keisha, "but she's running late. She called on her cell." She slipped onto the bench beside Megan and propped her own knapsack and the one she used in the play on the sidewalk at her feet.

Lizzie tapped Cindy to translate Lizzie's sign language into words and then she said, "Keisha, you were so funny today. In rehearsal? When you fell down?"

"I fell down on purpose," said Keisha. "That's what scarecrows do."

"I know," said Lizzie. "I said it was funny."

"Oh, I thought you meant I fell down for real," said Keisha.

"You made it *look* real," said Lizzie, "which is why it was so funny."

"Thanks," said Keisha, brightening considerably.

"I like the wobbly thing you do with

your legs," said Megan. "You act like you don't know if you can walk or not. That's really funny too."

"Am I doing it right?" asked Keisha.

"It's hysterical," said Megan. "I'm supposed to hold you up, but I can't help laughing."

"Don't drop me," said Keisha, "or I'll really fall."

"That would not be good," said Megan.

Lizzie gestured for Alexis to push the plate of French fries closer to Keisha. "Try the French fries," she said. "This place has great French fries."

"Thank you," said Keisha, nibbling one with a smile. "You guys are always hanging out over here. I was afraid to come over before."

"Why?" said Megan. "We're friends!"

"We're friends, but you're kind of your own clique," said Keisha.

"No, we're not," said Alexis.

"The Leading Ladies, right?" said Keisha. "You even have a name."

"That was just a joke," said Megan. "You're in the play, right? That makes you a Leading Lady too. Anybody who sits with us is a Leading Lady."

"Get Tony Rosenblum over here," said

Cindy in her witchy voice—and all the girls gasped.

"There's that Wicked Witch again!" said Alexis.

"What Wicked Witch?" asked Keisha.

"The one that lives inside Cindy," said Lizzie. "She sneaks out anytime you don't know whether Cindy is being nice or not."

Even Cindy had to laugh at that remark. "I don't know what happens," she said. "These things just come out of my mouth."

Keisha smiled and reached for another French fry. She turned to Megan and said, "Is Solo coming to rehearsal tomorrow?"

"Ms. Scherer said not to bring him until we get to dress rehearsal," said Megan. "She says it's too much to manage a dog in rehearsal all the time. Which makes sense. But I still have to rehearse all his tricks with him when I get home every night to make sure he doesn't forget!"

"That was such a surprise when you brought him to the audition," said Keisha. "You remember when we were auditioning? And you wanted to be Dorothy? And you walked in with your dog?"

"Yeah," said Cindy. "That was pretty funny."

"What I meant to say," said Keisha, "was that I wanted to be Dorothy too."

"You did?" said Megan. "Wait. I knew that. Or, no—Cindy knew that. Somehow I knew that. But you never said anything at the time."

"I didn't put myself out there," said Keisha. "Now I know better—but now I'm happy being the Scarecrow. I didn't know that during auditions. All I knew then was that I really wanted to be you."

At first, Megan didn't know what to say. She knew about her own feelings—and she knew about the feelings of the characters she played in the mirror—but she was becoming more aware of other people's feelings as well. Like Cindy's feelings about her new friendship with Lizzie at summer camp. And Alexis's feelings toward her little brother with autism. And all the girls who wanted to be Dorothy but didn't get to be Dorothy. And even Megan's brother, Matt's, feelings about—well, a whole lot of things.

Megan turned toward Keisha and spoke as she signed, to make sure she'd be understood. "When you auditioned with that ribbon wand," she said to Keisha, "and you did that beautiful dance?"

Keisha nodded. "What about it?" she said.

"That was amazing," said Megan. "I wanted to be you."

Keisha smiled.

Lizzie reached an arm across the table to get Alexis's attention. "I want to be you," she said in sign language.

"What did she say?" asked Alexis.

"She said, she wants to be you," said Cindy.

"Why?" asked Alexis.

Lizzie shrugged and signed, "Everything."

"She means everything about you," said Cindy.

"And I want to be you," said Alexis to Cindy, "'cause you say crazy things."

"And I want to be you," Cindy said to Lizzie, "'cause you say the right thing."

"And I want to be you," said Megan to Alexis, "'cause you have the French fries."

It was a silly game, but they kept it going around the table. It held their interest and made them smile and laugh. In fact, they were still laughing long after the last French fry was gone.

FOURTEEN
THE NUMBER 4
LEAP

At first it seemed as though the rehearsals were going to last forever, and then soon enough it seemed as though there wasn't enough time. Between the afternoon rehearsals, nightly homework, walking Solo, feeding Solo, training Solo, and the daily grind at school, the eight weeks flew—and not just for Megan, but for her entire family. In the week before the show opened, David picked up Megan from rehearsals on his way home from work. They came home on Friday afternoon to chaos in the kitchen.

"*Ouch*, Mom!" cried Matt. "Staple the paper! Not me!"

"Stand still," said Lainee, "and you won't get stuck!"

Matt was standing on a chair, wearing

what appeared to be 50 percent of a Tin Woodman costume. Two large panels were draped over his shoulders like a sandwich board. Lainee was wrapping poster paper around Matt's arms to make sleeves when Megan and her father walked into the room.

"How's it going?" asked David, somewhat tentatively.

"This was your idea," said Lainee, gesturing with frustration at the cardboard and the stapler.

"The Tin Woodman, right? It looks great!" said Megan. "But it's supposed to be silver, right?"

"I'm wrapping it in aluminum foil, I think," said Lainee. She lifted a box of aluminum foil from the counter and waved it lamely.

Matt turned to his father with puppy-dog eyes. "Help," he said.

David put down his briefcase and moved in closer to investigate the problem. "I think we can forget about the aluminum foil," he said, carefully removing the box from his wife's grip.

"Thank you," said Matt.

"I'm thinking instead we should just spray-paint the whole thing silver," said David.

"What?" cried Matt.

"After you take it off," David continued, "but first—the sleeves." He took the poster board from Lainee and wrapped it around his son's arm. In a quick move, he stapled the length of the coil so that Matt's arm was suddenly contained in a tube.

"Perfect, Dad," said Megan.

"I can't move my arm," said Matt.

"Stop complaining," said Lainee.

"I'm serious!" Matt urged, as David repeated the process on the other side. "My elbows are trapped. I can't bend my arms!" He flailed his arm helplessly and the whole family found themselves laughing at his dismay.

"Maybe the Tin Woodman doesn't need to bend his arms," Lainee declared. "Maybe he just needs to follow the Yellow Brick Road, get his heart, and bring that Dorothy home."

"What if he has to pick his nose?" asked Matt. He rattled his cardboard arms and tried to look as pathetic as possible.

David stood back to consider the costume. "You be the judge, Megan," he said. "You're in rehearsal. Does the Tin Woodman need to bend his arms?"

"Well," said Megan, "we hold hands when we're dancing, and a couple of times he hands me my basket."

David sighed. "Okay," he said. He opened a drawer, pulled out a pair of kitchen shears, and reached for Matt's arm.

"Ahhhhh!" Matt yelped, tugging his arm back.

"I'm not cutting your arm; I'm cutting the cardboard," said David. "I'll hinge it in the middle so you can bend your elbow and pick your nose."

"Just be careful," said Matt.

Megan watched as her father performed surgery on the costume.

"Who's playing the Tin Woodman anyway?" Matt asked Megan.

"Casey Waite," said Megan. "You don't know her."

"Is she nice?" said Matt.

"Nice enough," said Megan.

"That's good," said Matt.

"What do you care if she's nice?" asked Megan.

"'Cause the Tin Man is my favorite," said Matt.

"Okay," said Lainee, using her marine drill-sergeant voice. "You need to clear out of this kitchen so that I can start dinner."

As if on cue, Solo charged through the kitchen, pausing to leap against every individual—from Lainee to Megan to David to Matt and the Tin Woodman. Then he ran out of the kitchen, leaving behind a substantial trail of muddy paw prints.

"Tell me that did not just happen," said Lainee.

"It didn't happen, Mom," said Megan—but it was too late. Lainee was already headed to the window over the kitchen sink. She peered into the backyard and cried, "Oh, no!"

Sure enough, Solo had dug up the flower beds again. Clumps of soil were tossed all over the place, and Lainee's carefully planted begonia bulbs were scattered left and right.

"Don't tell me," said David, as they inspected the crime scene. "Your brand-new begonias."

"Two trays of them," said Lainee, "in nice even rows."

Matt and Megan held back a few feet, standing apart in the grass. Lainee turned to face them. "You promised you'd keep Solo under control," she said.

"Mom, we never said 'under control,'" said Matt. "We said we'd train him."

"He's allowed to make mistakes," said Megan.

"Only so many times," said Lainee.

"I don't blame the kids," said David. "It's my fault. Solo is too much dog for our household."

"Our house is big," said Megan. "How can a dog be 'too much' for this house?"

"Dogs need a lot of space," said David.

"And some dogs just can't be trained," said Lainee.

"But we've been training Solo," said Megan.

"It's true," said Matt. "Megan and I have trained him to do lots of tricks. We just haven't trained him to stop digging yet."

"Well, we'd better," said David. "He'll dig a hole under the fence and get away, if we don't."

"I'm not convinced we *can* train that dog," said Lainee. "I told you this was a trial period. I said we'd wait and see whether the two of you could handle that dog. But maybe it's time for your father and me to have a talk about that dog."

"His name is Solo, Mom," said Megan. "Stop calling him that dog."

"I know, 'Solo,'" said Lainee. "I'm sorry. Maybe I was wrong to think that you kids could train him."

"But we *have*, Mom!" said Megan.

"It's true," said Matt. "We've been feed-ing him every day and walking him, and we give him a bath once a week."

"And he does tricks!" said Megan. "Matt helped me teach him because Solo does tricks when he plays Toto onstage! I was keeping it a surprise until opening night—but—he's not just in the show, he does *tricks* in the show!"

"It's true, Mom," Matt repeated.

"We can show you right now!" Megan exclaimed.

A few moments later, David and Lainee sat on patio chairs and waited while Megan paraded Solo into the yard. Megan had con-scientiously taken a few minutes to clean the mud off his paws with an old towel so that the dog would make a better impression on her mother.

"And now," said Matt, using his best ringleader voice, "I'd like to introduce Megan and her amazing dog!"

Matt and David shook their hands in the air, which was sign language for applause. Lainee did not.

Megan rolled up her sleeves and flexed her knuckles. Then she gently tapped Solo on the nose to get his attention, and she made the sign for "lie down." Solo lay down.

Megan signed "roll over."

Solo rolled over.

Megan signed "sit" and Solo sat. She signed "shake hands," and Solo extended a paw. She signed "walk" and Solo accompanied her about the yard. She signed "be gentle" and Solo gently took his favorite toy—a slobbery plastic dog bone—from her hand. She signed "drop it" and he dropped it. She signed "time for bed" and Solo curled up on his side, pretending to sleep.

If Solo had been taking a test in dog obedience, he would have passed with flying colors. "I am very impressed," said David.

"Okay, you did it," said Lainee. "I have to agree."

"Wait," said Megan. "There's one more trick, and it's the best one."

"And now, ladies and gentlemen," said Matt, shouting through cupped hands, "Solo will attempt the amazing, the stupendous, the death-defying—Number Four Leap!"

Matt played a drumroll on the back of a patio chair while Megan stepped into position with a great deal of drama. She stood on her right leg with her left foot crooked up to her knee—so that she formed a number 4 with her legs. She clapped her hands in front of her and—right on cue—Solo jumped through the hoop between her knees.

"Ta-da!" cried Matt.

"Okay, okay," said Lainee, breaking into applause herself. "Now I'm impressed. I am very impressed."

"He almost knocked me over a couple times," Megan explained, "because he's almost too big to jump through my legs. But I guess I'm getting bigger too." Solo ran about the yard, barking merrily, and returned to Megan. She dropped to one knee and gave him a hug. "Solo does the tricks because he loves me and—I'm not stupid—he does it for the snacks," Megan explained, "but he's a really good dog, and I know we can train him to be better!"

"Solo's not going anywhere," said David. "Don't worry about it. He's staying. Anyway, where would he go? He opens in *Wizard!* next week, isn't that right?"

"Dress rehearsal is on Thursday and we open Friday night," said Megan. "Two shows on Saturday. And then we close."

"Maybe there'll be an agent in the audience, and Solo will land a big Hollywood contract," said Lainee. "But if not, he stays with us. And can we please do something about the dog and the digging? I don't want to have to give up gardening because of Solo."

"We need to tackle the digging," David said to Megan and Matt. "I don't want to come home and find a hole under the fence."

"Whoa," said Matt. "Prison break. A runaway."

"If he digs deep enough, it could happen," David warned.

"We'll do it, Dad," said Megan. "As soon as possible, I promise!"

"Yeah, sure Dad, whatever, right," said Matt with a shrug.

"What did you say?" said David.

"I said we'll do it," Matt replied.

"And when?"

"Dad, I don't know," said Matt. "You gotta let me look the lesson up in the dog book first!"

"Just do it!" said David, as he followed Lainee inside.

Megan gave Matt a look that said, "Please don't talk back to Dad."

Matt's look back said, "Whatever."

FIFTEEN
THE SNEAKY PART

Alexis says you were an actress," Megan said to Mrs. Lopez.

"I *am* an actress!" Mrs. Lopez replied. "I got married and had kids and now I'm a mom. But that doesn't mean I stopped being an actress."

The technical rehearsal had come to a momentary standstill.

Ms. Scherer and Mr. Ryan, the science teacher who had gotten roped into doing their lighting design, were trying to solve a problem onstage. A certain lighting effect was supposed to look like clouds—so that it would seem as if the Winged Monkeys were flying when they were actually just standing in place, flapping their arms. But the lamp wasn't working and the Monkeys looked pretty stupid without it. Ms. Scherer and Mr. Ryan were onstage surrounded by Winged Monkeys, trying to fix that particular problem.

Megan used the break to head backstage. Her mom was making adjustments to the Munchkins' costumes in the room designated for the wardrobe. Unfortunately, Lainee was quite preoccupied when Megan poked her head into the doorway. She tried to talk with two safety pins in the corner of her mouth while tugging on the waistband of the Mayor of Munchkinland, who held onto a tabletop for balance.

Megan decided to visit Mrs. Lopez in the dressing room. Mrs. Lopez traveled with a large-sized fishing-tackle box that she had placed on top of the counter. The box opened to display several different trays with little compartments—and each compartment was filled with some tool she used for makeup. Creme sticks, mascara brushes, lipsticks, eye shadow, and tiny canisters of rouge.

"Are you being nice to my Enrique?" said Mrs. Lopez.

"I like Enrique," said Megan. "We don't talk much, but I like him."

"Be nice to him," said Mrs. Lopez. "He's a good boy, but he's shy."

"He's not that shy," said Megan. "He has the first line in the play, so he can't be that shy." Enrique was playing Uncle Henry, and he opened the play by calling for Dorothy to come in from the cornfields.

"Oh, I know," said Mrs. Lopez. "Every time I hear him onstage, saying that line—'come in from the cornfields!'—it makes me want to cry. He won't tell you but he's really very nervous about it. So be very nice to him."

"Where were you an actress?" asked Megan enthusiastically.

"I was in plays in college," said Mrs. Lopez. "And then I had friends in college who made little movies. Short films. And then I took a job on a boat—I was an actress and a singer. And I was in plays in theaters."

"And what was that like?" said Megan, all hushed and starry-eyed.

Mrs. Lopez turned as though she was surprised by the question. She looked down at the girl sitting on the folding chair in the tiny dressing room—and then she laughed. "It was wonderful!" she said, shaking off the memories. She waved her hands, shooing

Megan out of the room. "Off you go,
Dorothy! I think they need you back
onstage."

After the last Saturday rehearsal, almost
every kid in the cast was crowded around
the picnic tables at the Hot Dog Joint—and
everyone had French fries.

"So I hate to say, 'I told you so,' but I
told you so," said Casey.

"I told you so—what?" asked Cindy.

"I told you the whole *Wizard!* thing was a
trick," Casey replied.

"What kind of 'trick'?" asked Megan.

"Ms. Endee tricked us into reading a
book," said Casey. "That's what I said at the
beginning—and that's what I'm saying
now."

"Big deal," said Tony Rosenblum. "It
was a good book."

"Casey, are you still complaining about
reading a book?" crowed Megan. "You need
to get over it already!"

"It's not just that we had to read a
book," said Casey. "It's the whole *Wizard of
Oz* thing!"

"*What* whole *Wizard of Oz* thing?" asked
Megan.

"I know what she means," said Lizzie.

"Hey, Casey," said Cindy. "Lizzie says she knows what you mean."

"You do?" asked Casey. No one ever agreed with Casey, so she didn't know how to act when it happened.

"Sure," said Lizzie. "You mean almost every subject that Ms. Endee teaches has got something to do with *The Wizard of Oz*."

"Is that true?" said Megan.

"Haven't you noticed?" said Lizzie. "What are we studying in science?"

"It's been all animals, vegetables, and minerals," said Tony.

"Right," said Lizzie. "And what's an animal in *The Wizard of Oz*?"

"The lion," said Ronnie. "That's me."

"And what's a vegetable?" Lizzie continued.

"You mean like straw?" said Keisha.

"Straw or corn or whatever they stuff you with," said Lizzie. "And what's a mineral?"

"Is the Tin Woodman a mineral?" asked Casey.

"Yeah, metal is a mineral," said Tony.

"So the Lion, the Scarecrow, and the Tin Woodman are 'animal, vegetable, mineral'?"

asked Alexis. "Were we supposed to know that?"

Lizzie shrugged. "I don't know," she said, "but it's there."

"Is that what you meant?" Tony asked Casey.

"I guess so," said Casey. "Yeah, that's what I meant."

"Lizzie is really smart," Megan announced to the group. "Isn't my friend Lizzie smart?"

"And we get those questions in math class about how many yellow bricks does it take to build a road," said Alexis.

"*The Wizard of Oz*, again," said Lizzie. "It's everywhere."

"So Ms. Endee was just being funny with that question?" asked Megan.

"No," said Lizzie, "she was being sneaky! 'Cause she's trying to teach us something!"

"And all that stuff about the color spectrum and the frequency of green?" said Tony. "And the whole Emerald City thing?"

"See how sneaky she is?" said Lizzie, peering down the length of a French fry. "That's how Ms. Endee teaches!"

Word quickly spread to the other table about Ms. Endee's sneaky plan to make them learn something by reading *The Wizard of Oz*. Soon enough, every kid in class knew. But nobody seemed to mind.

Megan was still holding court at her table, laughing with friends about funny things that had happened in rehearsal. Like when Frankie Adams accidentally knocked over the Wicked Witch's castle. Or when Tony Rosenblum had been asleep with his nose buried in a comic book on Auntie Em's front porch while the scenery had rolled onstage in the run-through. It wasn't all that funny in the re-telling, but it was outrageously funny at the time.

Another time, Megan and Bethany had been in the middle of a scene with Ronnie Jiu as the Cowardly Lion—and Megan had been reciting Dorothy's lines in sign language while Bethany recited them in spoken language. But they got confused and had been working off two different pages at the same time—so everyone got messed up. Again, it was hard to explain to anyone who hadn't been there, but it was impossibly hysterical at the time.

Megan was about to ask Casey if she had been onstage when they tried to open the door to the Emerald City—but the door was *stuck*—when all of a sudden Matt appeared at the window of the Hot Dog Joint, perched on the pedals of his bike. His hair was messed up from the ride, and he was clearly winded and out of breath.

"Megan!" Matt cried. "Jump on my handlebars! You'd better get home fast!" Megan had never seen her brother so upset.

"Why? What's the matter?" said Megan, a little frightened. "Are Mom and Dad okay?"

"They're fine!" said Matt. "It's Solo!"

"What happened to Solo?!"

"Solo is gone!"

SIXTEEN
MEOW

We think he's about two years old, but we're not entirely sure." Megan's father paced the linoleum floor. "We adopted him as a stray."

Megan charged into the kitchen to find her dad on the telephone and her mom busy at the computer. Megan jerked a thumb toward her dad and looked questioningly at her mother. "Who's he talking to?" she whispered.

"The police," Lainee replied.

"The police!" Megan repeated. "Did they find Solo? What happened?"

"No, Megan," her mother said reassuringly, "your father is filing a missing dog report—if there is such a thing. We're asking the police to keep a lookout. This way, if they see a dog that matches Solo's description, the police will know to bring him home to us."

"He's a mix," David continued into the phone. "Part German shepherd, part border collie. The vet thinks he's about two years old. Probably about forty pounds. Answers to the name Solo."

"The police are in their patrol cars on the streets a lot more than we are," Lainee explained. "And we want as many people looking for Solo as we can get."

"I saw the hole," said Megan. Once Matt had dropped his bike in the driveway, he had shown Megan the hole that Solo had dug in the dirt by their backyard fence. "He must have been digging for hours," Matt said, "and then he squeezed through that little hole." Megan shook her head to get rid of the image of Solo squeezing under the fence to escape.

"How come Solo wanted to run away?" she asked her mother.

"It's just something that happened, Megan," said Lainee. "I don't think he meant to run away. He might be trying to find home right now—but he got lost. Dogs dig because they dig."

"I saw this movie once, and that's how they got out of jail," said Matt. The whole family was now in the kitchen. "The prisoners dug and dug until they went under the wall."

"This was not a prison break, Matt," said Lainee. "It's just a lost dog."

"And he wouldn't be lost," said David, covering the receiver with one hand, "if you had trained him not to dig like you promised."

"I tried, Dad!" Matt protested. "Dogs don't learn overnight!"

"It's not your fault, Matt," said Megan.

"I'm sorry," said David. "You're right. I'm just worried about Solo."

"I hope nobody kidnaps him, or dognaps him, or whatever you call it," said Matt.

"Dognap?" said Megan, suddenly teary.

"Matt, you're not being helpful," said Lainee. She pressed a button on the computer, and the printer began to churn. Megan recognized Solo's face on the paper slowly emerging down the chute.

"What's that?" she asked.

"I downloaded a photo of Solo," said Lainee, "and put together a flyer so we could post a 'lost dog' notice around the neighborhood."

Lainee held up the printed page so that

Megan could see. It showed a large photo of Solo, smiling for the camera. "I remember when we took that photo," said Megan. "Remember, Matt?"

"The ice cube day?" said Matt.

It was the day that Megan and Matt tried to find out if Solo liked ice cubes. They scooped an ice cube out of the tray and offered it to Solo. The dog had licked the cube about two hundred times, trying to get it to melt.

"What was ice cube day?" asked Lainee.

"I'll tell you another time, Mom," said Megan. She felt too sad about the possibility of losing Solo to spend any time talking about all the good times.

In big block letters above the photograph, Lainee had typed the word "MISSING." Below were the words "If you find 'Solo,' please bring him home to 452 Morton Street."

"What do you think?" asked Lainee.

"Great, Mom," said Megan, "but you should add our telephone number."

"I didn't type our telephone number?" said Lainee, taking the paper to look for herself. "What do you know? I'm so upset that I forgot our telephone number." She returned to the computer and revised the page.

"I didn't think you liked Solo enough to be so upset," said Megan.

"Yes, I'm upset about Solo," said Lainee. "And I'm upset for you, Megan. I know how much you love that dog. And I love him too."

"Your mother is cranky about dogs," said David, "but she's a softie inside."

Megan leaned over the chair to watch as Lainee typed their phone number onto the flyer. "And describe him," said Megan. "Like Dad did on the phone."

"Good idea," said Lainee, typing the words "part German shepherd, part border collie."

"Okay, officer, yes, thank you very much," David said into the receiver. He hung up and put his hands on his hips. "How did that sound?" he asked.

"You did good, Dad," said Megan. "What do we do now?"

David shrugged and said, "We wait."

"No, we don't," said Lainee. "We have flyers to distribute around the neighborhood." She tapped the computer button again, and another page began to churn out of the printer.

"Can I help?" asked Megan.

"Of course you can," said Lainee. "We

can walk the neighborhood or maybe you can ride your bike. In fact, while I make copies on the scanner, why don't you hop on the Internet and send out an e-mail. Make sure all your friends know that we're missing our dog."

"But what can *they* do?" asked Megan.

"Keep an eye out," said Lainee. "Spread the word. Hit the streets."

Dear friends, I have sad news. Our dog, Solo, is missing. If you've met him already, you know that he's two years old and maybe forty pounds. If you don't know him, he is black and white with a big fluffy tail and surprisingly big feet. He is half German shepherd and half border collie, which makes him really smart and fast. He is also very nice and friendly so if you see him, you shouldn't be afraid. He will not bite you. He will probably lick you.

Please, please, please let us know if you find our dog.

Your friend, Megan.

P.S. I attached a photo of Solo with an ice cube in his mouth.

Lainee printed additional copies of the "lost dog" flyer. "I think twenty copies should do the trick," she said, turning toward Megan. "Should we go hang these up around the neighborhood?"

"Let's do it," said Megan. "Dad, do you want to come along?"

"I'll stay here in case anybody calls," said David. He was sitting by himself on the sofa in the den. He hadn't even turned on the television.

"Good thinking, Dad," said Megan. In truth, Megan wanted to curl up on the sofa next to her dad and keep her fingers crossed that the telephone would ring. She wanted to be there when the doorbell rang, and the police or some stranger showed up to return Solo. But there was no point in staying home as long as the flyers had to be posted about the neighborhood.

She hurried into the den to give her dad a hug and a kiss, and then she ran outside to catch up with her mother who was already headed toward the sidewalk with her flyers.

"Solo!" Lainee called out down the street, in case the dog was nearby and might hear. They waited a moment and then, when Solo didn't appear, they continued walking.

"I brought masking tape and I brought

a stapler," said Lainee, shaking her wrist to show off the roll of tape she wore as a bracelet and the black stapler that she held in her hand. "That way, we can staple them to telephone poles or tape them to lamp posts."

"Good thinking," said Megan.

"Are you worried about Solo?" asked her mom. "Being missing?"

"I wish he was at home," said Megan.

"Did your father seem okay?" asked Lainee.

"I guess so," said Megan. "I mean, he seemed sad."

They walked in silence for a few moments—except for the occasions when Lainee or Megan called out, "Solo!" Each time, they waited to see if Solo came charging out of the bushes or bolting around the side of a neighbor's house—and when he didn't, they kept walking. As they rounded the corner, they stumbled into Mrs. Applebee, a rather elderly woman who lived by herself in a house two doors down from the bus stop.

"Hello, Mrs. Applebee," said Lainee.

"Hello, hello," Mrs. Applebee replied. "How are you and Megan today?

Megan didn't feel like talking at the moment. She didn't want to be rude; she was just feeling shy. So she buried her head against her mother's hip and didn't say anything. Lainee stroked her hair. "Not so good, I'm afraid," Lainee explained to Mrs. Applebee. "We think our new dog, Solo, ran away this afternoon." She held out a flyer so that Mrs. Applebee could read the news for herself.

"Oh, dear," said Mrs. Applebee with genuine concern. "My dear husband and I once had a poodle named Ginger. That poodle was the smartest dog that ever lived—or so we thought. Then one day Ginger ran away. Oh, how I cried."

Megan winced. Mrs. Applebee's sad story was about the last thing she wanted to be told. She pulled away from her mother's hip to ask, "But Ginger came back, right?"

Mrs. Applebee shook her head in the negative. "Nope!" she replied. "She never did! I still get sad whenever I think about that sweet dog Ginger."

"Well, here," said Lainee, eager for Mrs. Applebee to finish her story and move along. Megan was already upset enough. She pressed the flyer into Mrs. Applebee's hand and said, "If you should happen to see Solo, please give us a call. We'll be right over."

"Oh, yes indeed," said Mrs. Applebee.

"Don't you worry," Lainee said to Megan, as they continued down the sidewalk. "Solo is going to turn up. Just you wait and see."

"If only I had brought Solo to rehearsal today," said Megan, "this would never have happened."

"Well, that's not entirely true," said Lainee.

"It was a tech rehearsal, and they said it was too crazy to have the dog around. But if he had been, he'd still be here!"

"Megan, Solo slipped through a hole he dug under the fence. It probably happened early this morning. We didn't notice that he hadn't touched his food until midafternoon. So it's nobody's fault—and we're doing all we can. Sometimes when you're upset, it's important to stay busy. No sense sitting around and worrying."

They stopped at a lamp post. Megan placed the stack of flyers on the sidewalk and lifted one into position against the pole. Lainee tugged the masking tape off her wrist and ripped off a strip to tape the flyer into place.

"You know what I like about you?" Lainee continued. "You notice how other people are feeling. You told your father he did a good job on the telephone, and that made him feel better. You told Matt it wasn't his fault when I know he's feeling guilty. And you didn't hesitate to help me with these flyers—because I really didn't want to be out here doing this alone."

"Yeah, it wouldn't be much fun doing this alone," said Megan. She let go of the paper once it was taped into place. "Besides, it goes faster with two." Megan picked up the stack of papers, and they continued down the sidewalk.

"Mom," she asked, "isn't it going to get dark soon?"

"That's why I want to make sure we get our flyers up while it's still light out," said Lainee. They stopped at a wooden telephone pole. Megan held the page in position while Lainee stapled.

"But what will we do if it gets dark, and Solo isn't home yet?" asked Megan.

"Animals are pretty good at taking care of themselves," said Lainee. "I'd be very surprised if he doesn't find his way home by dinnertime. But if he doesn't, we'll just have to say our prayers and hope he shows up in the morning."

"Will he do that?" asked Megan.

"He might," said Lainee. "When I was a little girl, we had a cat who kept running away. He went over the fence so many times that we called him Home Run. But the next morning, he was always there. Meowing for his breakfast on the back step."

Lainee meowed like a cat. She stroked her whiskers and licked her paws. Megan laughed.

"Solo doesn't like cats," said Megan.

"How do you know?" asked Lainee.

"He chased one once," said Megan. "Some cat that wandered into our backyard. It didn't realize we had a dog."

"But then it found out," said Lainee.

"In a big way," said Megan. She imitated Solo, barking loudly and chasing the cat after it intruded in their backyard.

"Maybe that's what happened," said Lainee. "Maybe Solo was chasing a cat and got lost. Maybe he's been chasing that cat this whole time."

"Maybe," said Megan.

They continued around the block until they came full circle back home, stopping every now and then to attach a flyer. Sometimes they meowed together like cats. And sometimes they both shouted, "Solo!"

"Mom, what do we do if Solo *doesn't* come back?" Megan asked when her mother stopped by her room later to tuck her in. "Like Mrs. Applebee's dog," she continued. "What if we never see Solo again?" Lainee smoothed her daughter's hair and brushed a tear off Megan's cheek with her thumb.

"Aw, honey," said her mother, "we have to stay positive. Solo will come back. He's probably a little turned around but he knows where he's loved, and he sure knows where he's fed. You'll see. You'll wake up in the morning and he'll be on the back porch, howling to get in."

"But what if he's not," said Megan.

"I think," her mother continued, in a soft bedtime voice, "that if you dream about Solo tonight, you should dream about him coming home. Not about him staying away. Because if you dream about him coming home, it's going to send out a signal—like a dog whistle—so he won't be lost. He'll know it's coming from home."

"There's no place like home," said Megan. "Click-click-click." She tapped her wrists together three times as though her hands were little ruby slippers.

Lainee kissed her on the forehead and turned off the light. She left the door ajar so that a sliver of light came in from the hallway, the way Megan always liked it. "I didn't tell anybody, but I've been knitting him a sweater," she added from the doorway. "And that's a big dog for a sweater."

When Megan was alone, she curled onto her pillow and tried to sleep but she couldn't help thinking about Solo—whether he was sleeping or where he was sleeping. Was he in an alley? Was he in someone's home? Maybe someone's car? She couldn't stop thinking about Solo.

The door opened a bit, casting light across Megan's face. She looked up to see her dad in the doorway. He stepped gingerly over Megan's homework, clothes, and toys to sit at the foot of her bed and tug on her big toe as he always did when he woke her up in the morning.

"Hey, tomato," he said, "you feeling sad?"

Megan nodded.

"Me too," said her dad. "But we have to keep our spirits up. Feeling sad isn't going to bring Solo home."

"Dad," said Megan. "What are we going to do if Solo doesn't come back?" It was a repeat performance but Megan wanted to know what her dad had to say. Sometimes, she found, if she asked the same question of both parents, she got two completely different answers. Sometimes it made sense, sometimes it didn't, and sometimes the real answer was sort of somewhere in between.

"Oh, he's coming back!" her father enthused. "I feel it in my bones."

"Mrs. Applebee's dog didn't come back," said Megan.

"Who is Mrs. Applebee?" asked David.

"That old lady down the street," said Megan. "She had a poodle. It ran away. She cried but it never came back."

"Megan, honey," her father continued, "I don't want you to worry about Mrs. Applebee and her dog. Our dog, Solo, is coming back; I just know it! I have a sixth sense about these things. If I lose my sunglasses or my car keys, sometimes I know they're gone. But other times, I think, *Oops,*

I just misplaced them; they're gonna show up. And that's the way I feel about Solo. He's going to show up. I just know it!"

"Are you sure?" said Megan, almost afraid to hope.

"Absolutely!" her dad said with conviction. "We haven't seen the last of that dog!"

"You're right," said Megan, almost in a whisper.

"I know I am," her dad insisted. "I know I am."

SEVENTEEN
COLD FRIES

The Leading Ladies met at the Hot Dog Joint for one last heaping cheese-covered plate of French fries between the end of the school day and the beginning of the *Wizard!* dress rehearsal— but none of the girls could even nibble on a single French fry because they were so upset about Megan's missing dog.

"My mom asked, 'What's the matter?'" said Alexis. "And I couldn't even tell her the story because I started to cry."

"And you hardly knew Solo," said Cindy.

"I met him," said Alexis. "I met him at the audition. I met him at rehearsals."

"Oh yeah," said Cindy, somewhat sheepish.

"Everybody met him," Alexis continued. "Everybody made a big deal."

"That's right," said Cindy. "I forgot."

"The idea of any dog disappearing like that!" said Alexis. "That's what makes me want to cry." She reached for a French fry and twirled it between her fingers.

"I know," said Lizzie. "You think it can't happen, and then it does."

"I don't even know what to say," said Cindy. "I've never been in this situation before."

"You're still not in this situation," said Megan. "He wasn't *your* dog."

"I didn't mean *that*," Cindy protested. "I only meant I don't know what to say to a friend who's lost a dog. I've never known anyone who's lost a dog before. My cousin lost her cat but nobody liked the cat very much anyway. Nobody liked my cousin that much either because he was always—"

Lizzie reached for Cindy's arm to get her attention. "Cindy," she signed, "this is about Megan. It's not about *you*."

"I know that," Cindy responded. "I'm only saying I'm as upset as anyone. I'm not being the Wicked Witch of the West! I'm just trying to say the right thing!"

"What did Lizzie just say?" Alexis asked, gesturing in Lizzie's direction.

"Alexis," Cindy snapped, "you really need to learn sign language if you're going to hang out with us because I can't be translating for you all the time."

Megan patted Alexis's arm. "She said, it's not about Cindy," she explained. "She said, it's about *me*."

"Oh," said Alexis.

The girls were quiet for a little while. Lizzie reached toward the plate of French fries and gently pressed her finger into some salt. Then she tapped her fingertip against the tip of her tongue.

"I can't believe we ordered these," said Alexis, still twirling her French fry. "I'm not even hungry."

"We ordered them because we always order them," said Cindy.

"Enough already," said Megan. She picked up a French fry and took a big bite. Everyone watched her chew. When she was finished, she swallowed hard and said, "Oh, great, delicious."

"Are they cold?" said Alexis.

"Do you think your dad would get another dog?" asked Cindy.

"Cindy!" all the girls cried—as if that was the absolute wrong thing to say.

Megan surprised them all by groaning loudly. "I'm so tired of feeling sad!" she said. "I just want to go across the street and get ready for this dress rehearsal and give the best performance I can give." She gathered her things, left the table, and walked out the door. Her friends watched through the window as Megan paused at the curb to look both ways before crossing the street.

"Wow," said Alexis, "I wouldn't be able to do anything if I found out my dog was missing."

"Good for Megan," said Lizzie. "The show must go on. I'll let Jann know we're leaving." Jann sat at the next table with her nose buried in a book"

"Should I wrap up the French fries in a napkin?" asked Cindy.

"Bring them for Ms. Scherer," suggested Alexis.

"Good idea," Cindy replied.

The dress rehearsal of *Wizard!* was a complete and total disaster. No one was on time, no one knew their lines, and no one knew when to get off the stage. Looking back after the run-through finally ended, the entire class was convinced that they were sitting on the biggest turkey ever seen in any school auditorium.

It seemed pointless to list what went wrong because everything that could go wrong *had*. None of the special effects worked. The tornado was late, the Yellow Brick Road was crooked, Emerald City was only half-green because they ran out of paint, and the Winged Monkeys never got off the ground.

The cast assured themselves that all the technical stuff would be fixed by opening night but, to make matters worse, the actors' individual performances were all over the place. The Scarecrow didn't have a brain or enough straw. The Tin Woodman didn't have a heart or any pants. The Cowardly Lion didn't have a mane, a tail, or courage. The Wizard forgot his lines, the Munchkins were off-balance and off-key; and when it came time for the Wicked Witch to melt, Tracy froze. As things went from bad to worse, the cast backstage grew more and more punchy.

"This is humiliating," said Ronnie Jiu.

"We haven't even staged the curtain call

yet," said Alexis. They were supposed to rehearse their bows before they ever had an audience.

"I'm not going out there and taking a bow!" said Ronnie. "There might be second graders in the front row with tomatoes!"

Naturally, Lainee attended the dress rehearsal to help with the costumes, and Megan was standing next to her in the wings when the Wizard's hot-air balloon collided with the cornfields. Megan and Lainee exchanged a glance but neither of them said a word because they had to stay quiet backstage.

Even so, Megan thought, *What next?* She knew her heart wasn't in her own role that day either. Instead of performing with her own dog, Solo, as Toto, Megan was supposed to act with a small stuffed animal that Ms. Endee kept in her bottom desk drawer. The toy was a Teacher's Day gift from Donny Vargas's mother, and it wasn't even a dog. It was a pug-nosed cross between a hamster and monkey, with a heart-shaped tattoo that read: "I love you." Megan had to hold it by the tail and say, "Here, Toto! Here, Toto!"—when all she wanted to do was cry.

*

Most of the cast took the dreadful dress rehearsal in stride, laughing at the calamity and jokingly offering assurances that it would never happen again. But the fun and games ended when Ms. Scherer gathered the cast for "notes"—her critical comments about what went well, what didn't, and what needed work.

At first the cast thought Ms. Scherer might have been laughing too because of the way her shoulders bounced—but when she turned around, they could see that their teacher had been crying. *Seriously crying*, noted Megan. Jann stood solemnly at her side.

"I had such hopes that we'd pull this off," Ms. Scherer began, "but—at this point—I don't know." She gathered herself and referred to her notepad, gesturing vaguely as though she didn't know where to begin. "Okay, people!" she continued with gusto. "Memorize your lines! Memorize your dance moves!"

Some kids laughed nervously, reminded of all their mistakes—but laughter was probably not the right thing to do at the time.

Ms. Endee rose from her chair and glared at them sternly. "You need to take this seriously," she said, in sharp response to the laughter. "It may be funny to you, but it's not going to be funny to an audience— or your parents, taking pictures. People have better things to do than to watch you goof off onstage. And I won't let you embarrass this school."

It was quiet in the auditorium as the cast members took in what their teachers had said. Ms. Scherer let the uncomfortable moment sit for a while and then she continued in a softer tone. "Besides, you guys, everybody loves *The Wizard of Oz*. The audience wants to hear the story. They want to see *you* tell the story—and they want to see *you*, period."

Ms. Scherer dropped her pad and rubbed her face. "Today, we didn't see that," she said. "Today was—not worthwhile. I hope you guys can pull it together by tomorrow; I really do. But right now, I'm not so sure. Right now, I feel like I've done all I can."

By the end of her remarks, everyone in the production felt awful.

"It's true we didn't do our best," said Megan.

"When things started going wrong," said Cindy, "I did the wrong thing on purpose, thinking it was funny. I only made things worse."

"We weren't taking it seriously," said Alexis.

"No," Cindy agreed.

"And we need to," Megan asserted. "I feel rotten. We could have done a better job."

"You guys," said Lizzie, "when I was in *Alice in Wonderland* last year, our dress rehearsal was ten times worse than this. It will come together tomorrow night. You'll see."

"I hope so," said Megan. She and Cindy went back to the dressing room to claim their backpacks. Everything was perfectly quiet backstage, as though even the walls were ashamed of the performance. Even Mrs. Lopez, who was never short of something to say, went about cleaning the dressing-room counter without a single word.

Outside the auditorium, the kids hung out on the steps waiting for their parents to pick them up. Usually, there was a lot of laughter and singing and honking of horns as kids made their way to their parents' cars. But tonight, the mood was uncomfortably solemn.

"What's the matter?" asked Ronnie Jiu's mother, when he hopped into the van. "I thought you liked this show!"

"I do," said Ronnie. "Let's just get out of here."

Since they had both witnessed the disaster, Lainee didn't need to ask Megan what was wrong on the ride home. "It's not the first dress rehearsal to go badly," she said to Megan, "and it certainly won't be the last."

Megan was quiet.

"Everything will be different with an audience," her mom promised.

"Don't even talk about the audience," said Megan. "It makes me jittery in the stomach to even think about an audience."

"Those are called butterflies," said her mom. "Butterflies tickling you on the inside. It's not like being afraid; it's like being excited because you want everything to go well."

"I want it to go well," said Megan, "but right now, I'm just tired. And so are my butter-flies."

EIGHTEEN
BREAK A LEG

Look," said David, holding out his hands. "Green fingers."

Lainee made David stay up late the night before, spray painting the costumes green for the Emerald City, rigging the joints on the Tin Woodman's cardboard arms and legs, and adding a layer of shiny cellophane on the Good Witch of the North's garbage-bag gown. Lainee got up early to finish the Cowardly Lion's tail, spruce up the Wizard's top hat and tails, and add blue glitter to the Winged Monkeys' goggles. When David came downstairs and showed off his green fingertips, Lainee wagged her own back at him and said, "Lookie, lookie, mine are blue!"

Somehow, in addition to costumes,

Lainee got roped into baking goodies for the opening night reception for the *Wizard!* cast as well. She had baked cupcakes the night before but David had agreed to meet in the kitchen that morning to assist in decorating them with emerald green icing.

"I hope Megan develops a different interest next year," Lainee confided to her husband, as they frosted the three dozen cupcakes. "I don't know how many of these theater productions I can take."

"Next time," said David, "don't volunteer for costumes."

David and Lainee had a quiet laugh over that remark. "Remind me to remind Megan to not volunteer me for costumes," said Lainee.

"She's not up yet?" said David.

"I told you the dress rehearsal was a disaster," said Lainee. "I think she's sleeping it off."

At that moment, the telephone rang. Lainee put down her cupcake and reached to answer the phone. "Hello?"

"Lainee, it's Rachel Endee," said the voice on the phone.

"Oh, hello!" said Lainee. She mouthed the words, "Megan's teacher," to David. "I hope everything's all right?"

"I'm afraid we had one more unfortunate development overnight," said Ms. Endee. "You probably know Bethany, the girl who's been voicing Megan's lines in the play."

"Yes, Bethany came to Megan's birthday sleepover," said Lainee.

"Well, Bethany woke up with laryngitis this morning," said Ms. Endee. "She completely lost her voice."

"You're joking," said Lainee.

"I wish I was," said Ms. Endee, "but I just got off the phone with her. She sounds like a frog."

Lainee covered the receiver with her hand and told her husband what had happened.

"Perfect," said David. "Megan is going to totally freak out."

"Why is Megan going to freak out?" said Matt, who walked into the kitchen still in his pajamas with bed-head hair.

"The girl who speaks Megan's lines as Dorothy woke up with no voice," said David.

"I don't want to throw the cast off by recruiting someone who's playing another part," Ms. Endee said into the phone. "Worse comes to worst, I suppose Ms.

Scherer or Jann or I could read the role, but I worry that it would kill the spirit of the whole thing."

"I'll do it," said Matt.

"What?" said David.

"Hang on, Ms. Endee," said Lainee, covering the phone again. "What?" she repeated to Matt.

"I said, 'I'll do it,'" said Matt.

"Are you sure?" said David. "You'll read the lines while Megan plays Dorothy?"

Matt blinked two times. "I don't have to wear a dress, right?" he said.

"Let me check," said Lainee. She returned to the phone and asked. "My son, Matt, says he'll do it but he wants to make sure he doesn't have to wear a dress."

"No, he doesn't have to wear a dress," said Ms. Endee.

"No dress," Lainee reported to the kitchen.

"I'm in," said Matt.

"He's in," Lainee reported into the phone.

"Thank you, thank you, thank you," said Ms. Endee.

"No, thank *you*, Ms. Endee," said Lainee. "We'll see you tonight."

When Lainee hung up the phone, she

and David turned to smile at their son. "What did I just say yes to?" said Matt.

"It's just such a nice thing for a brother to do," said Lainee, draping an arm around his shoulders.

"Why are you being so nice?" asked Matt, suddenly suspicious. "Am I going to look like a total idiot or something?"

"No, not at all," said David. "You'll look like a hero. You're saving the day for your sister, Megan."

"I'm regretting this already," said Matt.

Megan slept late that morning. Even after she woke up, she scarcely knew what to do with herself until she left for the auditorium late that afternoon. She was grateful and relieved, of course, that Matt had stepped in for Bethany—but she made it clear in no unspecified terms that she wasn't so grateful that she would be making his bed.

"I sort of feel responsible for Solo getting out," Matt confessed in the kitchen when their parents weren't around. "I tried to teach him not to dig holes—but I didn't try all *that* hard. So I figure this is the least I can do to make up for, you know, losing—"

"Don't say 'losing Solo,'" said Megan. "I don't want to think about that."

"—to make up for him digging his way out," said Matt, correcting himself.

"Well, thank you," said Megan. She pulled a bound stack of pages off the counter. "Here's the script. Read it over and over—because I don't want to hear that you made a bunch of mistakes."

"You never say 'good luck' to an actor," Mrs. Lopez explained, as she rubbed her thumb into a cake of rouge and dabbed the color onto Megan's cheekbones. "'Good luck' is bad luck. You're supposed to say 'break a leg' instead."

Megan cocked her head to one side. "'*Break a leg*'?" she repeated.

"That's backward, right? Isn't that the opposite of good luck?"

"Don't move," said Mrs. Lopez. She held Megan's chin to steady her face and studied Megan's makeup under the bright lights of the dressing room. "I can't explain it," she continued, "except that the theater is very superstitious." She reached for a zippered bag of makeup and sorted through various items until she located a zippered case with fresh cotton balls.

"Tell me more about the theater," said Megan.

"Megan," said Mrs. Lopez, "I've got fourteen other girls waiting in the hall with their mascara! I don't have time for the history of theater."

"But I want to know everything," said Megan.

"Go like this," said Mrs. Lopez. She opened her eyelids really wide and, keeping her chin down, she lifted her eyes toward the ceiling. When Megan imitated her, Mrs. Lopez leaned forward and took the mascara bottle from Megan's hand. She removed the brush from the cylinder and gently stroked it against Megan's lower lashes. She made Megan look to the left and the right as she applied more mascara to her upper lashes. She lifted Megan's chin so that Megan could read her lips, and she said, "Okay, blink."

Megan blinked four or five times, sitting very still.

"Beautiful," said Mrs. Lopez. She picked up a brown pencil and applied a few quick strokes to Megan's right eyebrow. She paused to inspect the results—and went to work on Megan's left eyebrow. As she did, she glanced down to make sure that Megan could see her lips. Then she said, "All I can tell you is that if you want to be an actress, you know it inside." She checked again to make sure Megan had been paying attention. Satisfied that she had, Mrs. Lopez patted her heart and said, "You know it here." She tapped her head as well and added, "And here."

Megan kept her eyes locked on Mrs. Lopez, waiting to be told more about the theater and how to become an actress. Instead, what Mrs. Lopez said was, "Lower your lip like this." Megan lowered her lip as Mrs. Lopez had done—and kept her face still while Mrs. Lopez applied a quick touch of lipstick. When she was done, Mrs. Lopez touched Megan's chin so that Megan knew to relax.

Mrs. Lopez tugged the blue bows on Megan's pigtails until they were evenly tied. As she did, she spoke slowly and evenly without looking Megan in the eyes. "People will come backstage to tell you how much they enjoyed the show," she said. "When they do, don't tell them about the mistakes or whatever went wrong. Don't ruin the show. Instead you say, 'Thank you! Thank you very much!'"

"Thank you," Megan repeated. "Thank you very much!"

"Good," said Mrs. Lopez. "You learn fast." She tugged the plastic top off a canister of hair spray and tilted Megan's chin once more. "Not everybody knows how to take a compliment."

"Yes, Mrs. Lopez."

Mrs. Lopez aimed the hair spray at Megan's pigtails. "Now close your eyes," she said. Megan closed her eyes and held her breath while Mrs. Lopez sprayed her hair. She felt the spritz of mist shower her head and held her breath so that she wouldn't inhale the fumes. When she felt a tap-tap on her shoulder, Megan opened her eyes to find Mrs. Lopez smiling at her.

"Now go break a leg," said Mrs. Lopez.

Megan returned to her spot in the girls' dressing room to find a number of small presents waiting on her chair. There was a funny postcard from Ronnie Jiu, a bag of green jelly beans from Alexis, a big green carnation from Keisha, a silly flamingo pen from Casey, a little wind-up toy from poor, sick Bethany, and a big yellow brick from Tony Rosenblum. Lizzie had left behind a small envelope addressed to Megan. When she opened it, glitter fell onto the countertop. Megan smiled warmly when she pulled out a small card that read: "Sparkle says, 'Shine!'"

"Omigosh," said Megan. "I'd better deliver my gifts!"

She reached for her backpack to retrieve the opening night presents she had prepared for her friends. She had folded simple pieces of purple origami paper to look like little houses. In case the shapes weren't obvious enough, Megan had written on the side of each house the word *"H-O-M-E."*

Jann poked her head around the door of the girls' dressing room and flickered the lights to get Megan's attention. "Ten minutes till curtain!" she said and disappeared behind the door.

Megan jumped from her seat. She cried, "Jann!" and opened the dressing room door so that she was face-to-face with her translator. "Jann, don't go anywhere!" she declared.

Jann was wearing a headset and carrying a clipboard. She froze in her tracks. "Is something wrong?" she asked.

"Just don't go," said Megan.

She darted back into the dressing room and grabbed one of the origami houses marked "HOME." She cupped it in the palm of her hand like a fragile egg and carried it into the hall. "Here, Jann," she said, "break a leg!"

"Thanks," said Jann with a smile. She placed the house so that it balanced on her clipboard if she carried it flat—and continued down the hall, turning back to shout, "Nine minutes till curtain!"

Megan's origami houses were a big hit—even in the boys' dressing room. Megan quickly returned to the girls' dressing room and sat at her mirror in costume and make-up. She had already checked her props the way Ms. Scherer had instructed them to do—especially the sapphire slippers, which were perfectly purple, and placed them on the fake wicked witch's legs where she would need to find them later. She returned to the dressing room and watched the girls behind her bustling in the mirror, searching for costumes, struggling into shoes, chattering excitedly.

Megan was all set. She had nothing to do but study her script one last time. She flipped through the pages, refreshing her memory of what to do and when. Other kids had costume changes or breaks between scenes—but once Megan hit the stage as Dorothy, it was go-go-go.

She felt a rush of nerves, a flutter of those butterflies in her stomach—and she quickly shook her hands to get rid of the jitters. While she did, she happened to notice herself in the mirror.

It was a simple mirror—just like the one in her bathroom where she had done all her playacting until now. The obvious difference was that Megan didn't have to stand on a stool and lean over the sink to pretend she was Dorothy. And the bigger difference was *The Wizard of Oz* wasn't going to happen in the mirror. This was a real play—happening on a real stage—with real costumes, real lights, and real applause.

Megan was still lost in her thoughts when she felt a tap on her shoulder. Looking up, Megan saw that Jann was gazing at her in the mirror. "Two minutes till curtain," she said. "Ms. Scherer says, 'Places.'"

"Hey Pigtail-head," said Matt, when he saw Megan in the hallway backstage.

"The name is Dorothy, and you'd better get it right," said Megan.

"You'd better be grateful I'm reading your lines," Matt insisted.

"I said, 'Thank you!' Didn't I say, 'Thank you'?" said Megan, tugging playfully on Matt's jacket. "How many times do I have to say, 'Thank you'?"

"Every single day for the rest of your life," said Matt.

"If I say, 'thank you,' you have to say, 'you're welcome,'" said Megan.

"You're welcome," said Matt. "But let's not make this a habit."

"Hey!" she whispered, "I know where there's a hole in the curtain, and we can peek at the audience."

"Cool," said Matt.

All the other kids backstage were frozen in silence because Mr. Smelter, the school principal, was greeting the audience in front of the big curtain. Megan couldn't hear the announcement, so she didn't really care. She tugged on Matt's jacket until she found the spot in the velvet curtain that had the tiny hole. She pulled the fabric taut and pressed her eye against it.

"Hey, don't hog," Matt whispered, pressing close beside her—but Megan suddenly pulled back with a look of alarm on her face.

"What's the matter?" asked Matt.

"Look for yourself!" said Megan. "Mom's in the third row!"

Matt peered through the hole and searched the audience. Sure enough, his mom sat in the third row as Megan said. Then he noticed the empty chair beside her.

Their dad wasn't in the audience.

Matt pulled back and looked at his sister. "No dad," said Megan, her lip trembling with concern. "The play's about to begin— and *no dad.*"

Matt shook his hands to let Megan know that the sound of applause had filled the school auditorium. Clearly, Mr. Smelter had finished his announcement, and the show was about to begin. The stage lights bumped up, harsh and bright. The curtain hadn't been raised yet—but the tasseled fringe had begun to stir.

If Matt hadn't pushed Megan in the right direction, she might have missed her entrance altogether.

The show had begun.

NINETEEN
THE NICK OF TIME

The red stage curtains opened on the cornfields of Kansas.

Of course, it wasn't really the cornfields of Kansas. It was what Ms. Scherer called an optical illusion. The backdrop was painted to look like rolling hills and cornfields as far as the eye could see. Katherine, Elizabeth, *and* Lillian had teamed up to make the surface look like real cornstalks and grass. The blue sky above the cornfields was equally impressive. Daybreak dawned on the horizon. Crows circled above the corn. The skies were wide and clear over Kansas, except for a distant glimpse of cumulonimbus clouds.

The stage area was supposed to be the farmyard with a segment of fencing and a few scrawny trees. It amused Megan and the other students that the audience had no idea the trees were only one-sided. They had built them out of cardboard boxes, paint, tissue paper, and glue—taking time to write their names on the "upstage" side of the tree trunks for good luck.

Auntie Em's porch and a partial view of the house peeked in from the far side of the stage. A wheelbarrow was positioned in the middle of the yard to make it look as if this was really a working farm.

Apart from the props and scenery, the stage was empty when the curtain went up. After Enrique crossed the stage as Uncle Henry, shouting, "Dorothy, Dorothy! Come in from the cornfields!" Dorothy was supposed to run onstage from the cornfields calling for "Auntie Em"—but Megan had been told to wait and count, One-one-thousand, two-one-thousand, three before making her move.

She was standing in the wings next to Cindy, watching anxiously as the stage lights illuminated the scenery. In the shadows backstage, they were surrounded by Munchkins who weren't scheduled to enter until the second scene but were too excited to wait in their dressing room. Cindy was in the habit of counting off the "one-one-thousand" with Megan and giving her a little push onto the stage—but Cindy faltered on opening night. For some reason, she wasn't counting.

"What's the matter?" asked Megan.

Cindy shook her hands in the air and said, "The audience is clapping! They're clapping for the scenery!" Megan peeked into the audience as much as she dared and, sure enough, they were applauding. Several Munchkins patted Megan on the back for good luck without realizing that they were crowding her onto the stage. In the excitement, Megan and Cindy had forgotten to do the "one-one-thousand" count, but Megan figured, *What the heck.* She went ahead and ran onstage.

For a moment, she forgot what to do when she got there. Suddenly the lights were much brighter than they'd ever been in rehearsal. The colors in the costumes and the scenery were twice as vibrant in the light. The biggest surprise was that she couldn't see the audience. At first, in the glare of the stage lights, the audience was simply a big black wall.

In a blink, the moment passed and

Megan ran toward the front porch of Auntie Em's house as she had been instructed to do. Ms. Scherer had called it her "blocking." It meant where she entered, and where she went, and where she went after that—all the way until she exited the stage again.

"Auntie Em! Auntie Em!" Matt was positioned on a chair just past the edge of the stage where he recited the lines that Megan was performing in sign language.

Megan rang a cowbell dangling off the front porch and tapped on the painted windows till Auntie Em appeared onstage. Of course, it wasn't really Auntie Em. It was Alexis. She looked a little scared because of the audience and everything, but Megan took her hand reassuringly and pulled her farther onto the stage. She patted Alexis's hand as if to say, *Come on, it's all make-believe. We've done this a thousand times already. We know what to do.*

Dorothy and Auntie Em had a little scene before the tornado struck. Actually, Auntie Em did most of the talking. They discussed whether Dorothy had finished her chores, the condition of the scarecrow in the field, and the whereabouts of Toto. During the conversation, Dorothy scrambled about the yard to finish her chores, propped up the weather-beaten scarecrow in the corn patch, and searched the yard for Toto. Auntie Em had a few comments about what a good girl Dorothy was—and then all of a sudden, they both noticed the tornado.

While Megan and Alexis were handling the scene, Megan noticed an unusual amount of commotion among the Munchkins in the wings, who seemed to be running about and bumping into curtains. Megan chalked it up to opening-night jitters. During rehearsals, Ms. Scherer had coached the Munchkins to be quiet and still backstage but maybe opening night was different because of all the excitement. As the scene progressed, Megan followed her blocking and went to the corner of the porch where Toto was supposed to run into her arms. They had re-worked the scene after Solo had disappeared. It used to be that Solo ran into Megan's arms and then Megan got Solo to do a few tricks. But now, Megan was supposed to notice the stupid stuffed animal that was the new Toto and run to retrieve it from beside the wheelbarrow. She was supposed to kiss it on the nose and tuck it under her arm, and that was that. It wasn't like the thrill of having a real dog onstage but what could she do? *I can't think about Solo right now,* Megan warned herself. *If I start thinking about Solo, I'll never get through the show.* And, as Ms. Scherer had said, "The show must go on."

Megan reached the spot at the end of the porch and turned on cue to call for "Toto"—but when she did, her jaw fell open.

Her father, David, was standing in the wings. He held a dog leash—and at the end of the leash was *SOLO!*

When David unclipped the leash from the collar, Solo bolted across the stage. He jumped onto Megan's costume, leaped in circles about her, and then jumped onto her costume again, barking loudly. Megan dropped to her knees and wrapped her arms around Solo's neck—which put her in the perfect position for Solo to smother her with dog kisses, licking her face over and over and over again.

From the side of the stage, Matt continued to read Dorothy's lines. "There you are, Toto," he said. "Don't scare me like that."

Alexis rang the cowbell on the front porch to get Matt's attention. When Matt finally turned, Megan was smiling in his direction with one arm wrapped around the dog and one finger pointing demonstratively at Solo's head.

"Look, Matt! Solo! I mean—Toto!" Megan blurted out loud. "He's back!" Megan screamed with joy.

Matt wanted to ask all the questions— what and how and where and who—but the play was under way, so he knew he couldn't talk about it now. Instead, he simply repeated Dorothy's line, only this time with feeling. "There you are, Toto!" he said with gusto. "Don't scare me like that!"

Megan laughed. Looking into the wings, she saw her dad signing a quick message— "He came home somehow! I found him in the backyard! Long story! I'll tell you later!" All the Munchkins were cheering. Ms. Endee and Jann raised their joined hands and shook them together like prizefighters, overjoyed at Solo's happy return. Megan also saw Ms. Scherer, smiling too, but pointing emphatically at the play script in her other hand.

The show must go on, thought Megan. She gave Solo another good hug and jumped to her feet. Ms. Scherer, Ms. Endee, and Jann shared a collective sigh, relieved that the play was back on track. But then—instead of following her blocking—Megan ran to the center of the stage and gestured for Solo to follow her.

"Oh dear," muttered Ms. Endee. She and Ms. Scherer exchanged a puzzled look, uncertain as to what kind of stunt Megan might pull now.

First, Megan got Solo to focus his attention on her. She placed two extended fingers of her right hand across two extended fingers on her left hand, with both palms facing down. It was sign language for "sit"—and Solo promptly sat down. There was a mild smattering of applause from the audience.

Megan held Solo's attention. She laid her cheek against her right palm—sign language for "lie down"—and Solo promptly lay down on the stage.

Megan circled behind the dog to make sure he stayed in place. Then she got his attention again and rolled her wrists one over the other. It was no surprise to anyone when Solo began to roll over on the stage. The audience responded enthusiastically to this good trick. But Megan wasn't finished.

She brought Solo back to the front porch. Then she ran downstage and jumped into position like a cheerleader with her hands poised at her hips. Holding her balance, Megan cocked one foot beside the knee of her other leg so that her legs formed a perfect number 4.

And that's when Solo took a running start from the porch and charged directly toward the front of the stage—cleanly jumping straight through the "hoop" formed by Megan's legs. Megan wobbled slightly but managed to keep her balance. After this trick, Solo leaped about barking, clearly proud of himself. Megan laughed, and the audience cheered.

"Come on, Toto," said Megan, reaching for Solo's collar. "We'd better run and hide from the tornado!"

Megan had clearly jumped half a page forward in the official play script but it didn't really matter. Matt simply repeated the line that Dorothy had just spoken, with pointed emphasis. The technical crew backstage jumped on the cue and began to shake the metal sheet that served as a thunder maker, trigger the sound effects, and flicker the lights. And Megan and Solo jumped onto the front porch as it began to roll offstage.

The audience applauded wildly.

The cast of Munchkins charged onstage

with long strips of purple, blue, and silver fabric and ran in three different circles onstage—one headed clockwise and two headed counterclockwise. With the excitement of the lights and the music, it looked like a tornado—especially because the Munchkins made a lot of scary noises as if they were riding a roller coaster. Somewhere in their midst, Tony Rosenblum appeared with a long stick that held a cardboard model of Dorothy's house. It swooped and swirled overhead as though it was caught in the storm. Several boys ran along the outer rim of the circles, ringing bells and beating drums.

After a minute or so, the Munchkins dove underneath the purple fabric and huddled in hidden clumps on the ground. The boys with the bells and drums ran offstage. With a quick yank, the stage crew pulled away the cornfield to reveal a new backdrop. It depicted a multicolored rainbow that tracked a tremendous arc across the entire stage. Dorothy's house rolled back on—looking a little worse for wear from the storm—and the lights came up on Megan and Solo, standing center stage.

Only they weren't in Kansas anymore.

TWENTY
THE SHOW
MUST GO ON

Wizard! went off like gangbusters, with only a few goof-ups along the way.

Cindy got into a tangle with the Winged Monkeys. They had been staged to scurry backward onstage—with each monkey tugging on the next monkey's tail, like the playground game of cracking the whip. Unfortunately, an overexcited monkey behind Cindy tugged a bit too hard—and just as Cindy was entering the stage, she toppled over backward onto the floor. Oncoming monkey after monkey landed right on top of her. It was a total pile-up, only instead of kids, it was kids playing monkeys.

Fortunately, Cindy was a total trooper.

She scrambled to her feet, adjusted her winged monkey goggles, and got into position in time to flap her wings for the big special effect when the monkeys flew through the clouds. The spectacle of all the winged monkeys suddenly in flight came as such a surprise that the audience burst into spontaneous applause—which made all the monkeys grin.

A moment of panic happened backstage when the twinkling lights in Lizzie's Good Witch gown stopped working. Apparently, the battery had died. Fortunately, Jann had a spare battery ready and reconnected Lizzie only seconds before her big entrance into Munchkinland. Lizzie snuck into position on the upstage side of a set of wooden steps—and descended before the audience as though she was floating in a bubble. The Munchkins rattled jingle bells to heighten the effect. Halfway down the stairs, the strands of lights in her skirt began twinkling off and on—and several little girls in the audience gasped. Lizzie drew back her veil and waved her magic wand. "You must be Dorothy," she said in sign language. Her spoken voice was provided by three squeaky girl Munchkins speaking in unison, which added to the ethereal effect.

In the scene that followed, Lizzie went "up" on her lines, totally forgetting what she was supposed to say next. The sudden look of fright on Lizzie's face told Megan everything she needed to know—so Megan simply reminded Lizzie of the next line in sign language so that only they would understand. The scene continued without a hitch, except that Matt repeated the same line twice but nobody seemed to notice.

Tony Rosenblum had his fingers crossed in the wings when it came time for the Wicked Witch to melt. Tracy Benz moved into position in her big black garbage-bag witch gown. Megan grabbed a bucket, which was full of confetti because they didn't want to actually throw water onstage. She chucked the bucket at Tracy who let out a shriek and sank inside the folds of the gown until only her hat rested on top of the mound of black plastic. Megan got a big laugh when she tentatively poked at the hem of the dress with the tip of the witch's broomstick.

The main reason the actors knew the show had gone well was that the audience was especially quiet during the scene when Dorothy said good-bye to the Lion, the Tin

Woodman, and the Scarecrow. Ronnie dropped to all fours and rubbed his head against Dorothy's leg like a kitten. Casey shuddered and sobbed until her tin joints rusted tight. Then, for a little comic relief, Megan imitated Keisha's floppy legs as Dorothy approached the Scarecrow to say good-bye—but Keisha's legs didn't flop at all as she stepped confidently toward Megan and gave her a farewell hug. A heartfelt "awww" lingered over the audience.

It was only when the lights came up for the curtain call that the cast realized they had never staged their bows. The students crowded onto the stage with some understanding that the kids who had played the main characters should probably take their bows downstage in the middle. Cameras flashed across the audience as parents scrambled to take photos. Kids in the audience cheered for their favorites and booed for the Wicked Witch, even though they liked her a lot.

The cast invited Ms. Scherer, Ms. Endee, and Jann onto the stage and presented them with large bouquets of flowers. And when Megan, Solo, and Lizzie took their bows, the cast surprised them by raising their hands and shaking them in the sign for applause. Megan squeezed Lizzie's hand, and together, they smiled at the sight.

The audience caught on to the sign language for applause and shook their hands too—until the entire auditorium was shimmering with fluttering hands. Solo barked two or three times. Megan spotted Lainee, her mom, beaming at her from the third row. Just for Lainee, Megan pointed at the applause and quickly hooked her thumbs together and waved her hands like little wings. It was sign language for "butterflies." The sight of all the raised hands, wavering over the audience, looked just like a field full of butterflies.

Lainee blew her daughter a kiss, and Megan caught it with both hands.

Backstage was a mad dash of flowers and laughter and autographs for everyone. The Leading Ladies crowded in the doorway of their dressing room, black Sharpies in hand—ready to sign T-shirts or programs or anything at all for anybody in sight. Megan found Solo a warm corner under the countertop and commanded him to "stay" there to hide from the commotion. She found Matt in the hallway getting his T-shirt autographed by Enrique Lopez.

"Matt!" said Megan. "Where are Mom and Dad?"

"Coming down the hall," said Matt. "Where's Solo?"

"In the star dressing room," Megan replied, jerking a thumb over her shoulder. "He's waiting for you to tell him how good he was in the play."

Matt laughed and rushed into the dressing room to find Solo.

Megan looked up to see Lainee and David edging through the sea of students and parents, holding trays of cupcakes over their heads. She pointed the way into the girls' dressing room, and they managed to slip inside to find Matt with his arms wrapped around Solo's neck, getting smothered with wet-tongue dog kisses.

Lainee gave her daughter a big hug and a kiss once they were safely out of the crowd. "Megan, that was so exciting!" she said. "Your father and I are so very proud of you!"

"I'd hug you too," said David, trying to commandeer a secure spot on the countertop for the trays, "but my arms are full of cupcakes!"

Megan wrapped her arms around her father's waist anyway. "What happened with Solo?" she asked. "How did you find him?"

"It was Mrs. Applebee!" cried David.

"Mrs. Applebee took him?" asked Megan. That didn't sound right.

"No, Mrs. Applebee *found* him," her father replied. "I came home to a message on the answering machine in a little old lady voice—and I thought, *Who the heck is that?* Then I realized what she was saying, and I remembered what you had told me about Mrs. Applebee down the street."

"So what happened, Dad?" Megan urged.

"Apparently, Solo sat in Mrs. Applebee's driveway barking at the garage door all afternoon! She gave him a bowl of water and managed to tie him up in her backyard. Then she called us! Her message went on for a while about how scared she was to have such a big dog in her house. But when I drove over there, Mrs. Applebee was sitting on the sofa, and Solo was spread across her lap! She was feeding him little doggie treats left over from when she had that poodle! I don't think Solo wanted to come home!"

The family laughed—but Megan looked

at her father in disbelief. "But, Dad," she protested, "that still doesn't tell us what happened to him! Where did Solo go? What happened while he was gone?"

"Don't ask me!" said David. "Ask Solo!"

Megan turned toward the dog. "Solo!" she demanded. "Where'd you go? What happened to you?"

Solo barked loudly two times.

"I don't know what that means!" cried Megan. "You know I don't speak dog!"

The whole family laughed. "I guess we'll never really know where he went or what he did while he was gone," said Lainee. "I'm just glad he's back!"

"Me too," said Matt.

"Me three!" said Megan.

"Me four," added David. "But you're going to have to train him not to dig under the fence!"

"Oh, Megan! You were simply incredible tonight," said Lainee, wrapping her arms around her daughter once more. "I knew you were confident and I knew you were talented, but onstage—you were a powerhouse! And all those dog tricks too! You made us so very proud." She gave Megan an extra-specially tight squeeze.

"You made your mother cry; she was so happy," said David, wrapping an arm around Megan as well.

"You cried too," Lainee said to David.

"Okay, I got choked up too," Megan's father admitted, "but they were happy tears!" Megan and Lainee laughed.

"You mean I'm the only one who wasn't crying?!" cried Matt, leaning against Megan's makeup table. Lainee reached over to drag him into the family hug but Matt pulled away, protesting, "Oh, no you don't! You know I can't take all this lovey-dovey stuff!"

"Don't listen to him," said Megan, hugging her parents tighter. "I couldn't have done it without you, Mom and Dad."

"Hey!" said Matt, suddenly feeling left out.

"Or you, Matt!" added Megan. "You're the ones who've been incredible! The costumes and the cupcakes and helping with Solo—and all the rides in the car!"

"You're sweet," said Lainee, stroking Megan's hair, "but you know we'd do anything for you. Next year it might be gymnastics or cheerleading or karate. Who knows? We've already done the "school play" thing, so you might not want to do that again. But there's always horseback riding or tennis or maybe ballet. You know we'll get involved in anything you do."

Megan's jaw went slack. She looked at the makeup lights and the dressing-room mirrors and the racks of costumes behind her. She reached for the *Wizard!* program on her dressing table and held it up as evidence.

"Mom, you don't get it," she said pointedly. "I'm in the theater now! I'm doing *this* for life!"

Talk to the Hand:
Mega's Sign Language Alphabet

"Sit"

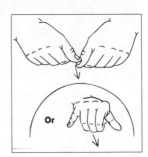

"Stay"

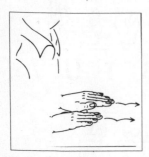

"I love you"

"Lie down"

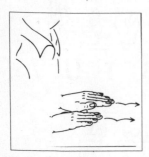

"Walk"